THE

GIRL

HE

CHOSE

(A Paige King Mystery—Book Two)

BLAKE PIERCE

Blake Pierce

Blake Pierce is the USA Today bestselling author of the RILEY PAGE mystery series, which includes seventeen books. Blake Pierce is also the author of the MACKENZIE WHITE mystery series, comprising fourteen books; of the AVERY BLACK mystery series, comprising six books; of the KERI LOCKE mystery series, comprising five books; of the MAKING OF RILEY PAIGE mystery series, comprising six books; of the KATE WISE mystery series, comprising seven books; of the CHLOE FINE psychological suspense mystery, comprising six books; of the JESSE HUNT psychological suspense thriller series, comprising twenty four books; of the AU PAIR psychological suspense thriller series, comprising three books; of the ZOE PRIME mystery series, comprising six books; of the ADELE SHARP mystery series, comprising fifteen books, of the EUROPEAN VOYAGE cozy mystery series, comprising four books; of the new LAURA FROST FBI suspense thriller, comprising nine books (and counting); of the new ELLA DARK FBI suspense thriller, comprising eleven books (and counting); of the A YEAR IN EUROPE cozy mystery series, comprising nine books, of the AVA GOLD mystery series, comprising six books (and counting); of the RACHEL GIFT mystery series, comprising six books (and counting); of the VALERIE LAW mystery series, comprising three books (and counting); of the PAIGE KING mystery series, comprising six books (and counting); and of the MAY MOORE suspense thriller series, comprising three books (and counting).

An avid reader and lifelong fan of the mystery and thriller genres, Blake loves to hear from you, so please feel free to visit www.blakepierceauthor.com to learn more and stay in touch.

BOOKS BY BLAKE PIERCE

MAY MOORE SUSPENSE THRILLER
NEVER RUN (Book #1)
NEVER TELL (Book #2)
NEVER LIVE (Book #3)

PAIGE KING MYSTERY SERIES
THE GIRL HE PINED (Book #1)
THE GIRL HE CHOSE (Book #2)
THE GIRL HE TOOK (Book #3)
THE GIRL HE WISHED (Book #4)
THE GIRL HE CROWNED (Book #5)
THE GIRL HE WATCHED (Book #6)

VALERIE LAW MYSTERY SERIES
NO MERCY (Book #1)
NO PITY (Book #2)
NO FEAR (Book #3

RACHEL GIFT MYSTERY SERIES
HER LAST WISH (Book #1)
HER LAST CHANCE (Book #2)
HER LAST HOPE (Book #3)
HER LAST FEAR (Book #4)
HER LAST CHOICE (Book #5)
HER LAST BREATH (Book #6)

AVA GOLD MYSTERY SERIES
CITY OF PREY (Book #1)
CITY OF FEAR (Book #2)
CITY OF BONES (Book #3)
CITY OF GHOSTS (Book #4)
CITY OF DEATH (Book #5)
CITY OF VICE (Book #6)

ADELE SHARP MYSTERY SERIES
LEFT TO DIE (Book #1)
LEFT TO RUN (Book #2)
LEFT TO HIDE (Book #3)
LEFT TO KILL (Book #4)
LEFT TO MURDER (Book #5)
LEFT TO ENVY (Book #6)
LEFT TO LAPSE (Book #7)
LEFT TO VANISH (Book #8)
LEFT TO HUNT (Book #9)
LEFT TO FEAR (Book #10)
LEFT TO PREY (Book #11)
LEFT TO LURE (Book #12)
LEFT TO CRAVE (Book #13)
LEFT TO LOATHE (Book #14)
LEFT TO HARM (Book #15)

THE AU PAIR SERIES
ALMOST GONE (Book#1)
ALMOST LOST (Book #2)
ALMOST DEAD (Book #3)

ZOE PRIME MYSTERY SERIES
FACE OF DEATH (Book#1)
FACE OF MURDER (Book #2)
FACE OF FEAR (Book #3)
FACE OF MADNESS (Book #4)
FACE OF FURY (Book #5)
FACE OF DARKNESS (Book #6)

A JESSIE HUNT PSYCHOLOGICAL SUSPENSE SERIES
THE PERFECT WIFE (Book #1)
THE PERFECT BLOCK (Book #2)
THE PERFECT HOUSE (Book #3)
THE PERFECT SMILE (Book #4)
THE PERFECT LIE (Book #5)
THE PERFECT LOOK (Book #6)
THE PERFECT AFFAIR (Book #7)
THE PERFECT ALIBI (Book #8)

TAKING (Book #4)
STALKING (Book #5)
KILLING (Book #6)

RILEY PAIGE MYSTERY SERIES
ONCE GONE (Book #1)
ONCE TAKEN (Book #2)
ONCE CRAVED (Book #3)
ONCE LURED (Book #4)
ONCE HUNTED (Book #5)
ONCE PINED (Book #6)
ONCE FORSAKEN (Book #7)
ONCE COLD (Book #8)
ONCE STALKED (Book #9)
ONCE LOST (Book #10)
ONCE BURIED (Book #11)
ONCE BOUND (Book #12)
ONCE TRAPPED (Book #13)
ONCE DORMANT (Book #14)
ONCE SHUNNED (Book #15)
ONCE MISSED (Book #16)
ONCE CHOSEN (Book #17)

MACKENZIE WHITE MYSTERY SERIES
BEFORE HE KILLS (Book #1)
BEFORE HE SEES (Book #2)
BEFORE HE COVETS (Book #3)
BEFORE HE TAKES (Book #4)
BEFORE HE NEEDS (Book #5)
BEFORE HE FEELS (Book #6)
BEFORE HE SINS (Book #7)
BEFORE HE HUNTS (Book #8)
BEFORE HE PREYS (Book #9)
BEFORE HE LONGS (Book #10)
BEFORE HE LAPSES (Book #11)
BEFORE HE ENVIES (Book #12)
BEFORE HE STALKS (Book #13)
BEFORE HE HARMS (Book #14)

CHAPTER ONE

Marta was fixing a faucet when she heard the noise.

She liked to think of herself as a personal assistant. That was what it said on her contract, and it was probably how Mrs. Estrom would have described her if she'd had cause to do so in company. That was the respectable term, the one that didn't make Mrs. Estrom feel like an old woman.

Marta knew the truth of it, though: most of the time, she was a glorified janitor and housekeeper. She cooked, she cleaned. She saw to the house and made sure that Mrs. Estrom had everything she needed in order to get on with her days without thinking about anything mundane. The formidable matriarch of the extended Estrom family had far better things to do with her time, spending it on everything from seeing important political figures to organizing elegant soirees.

Right now, she was asleep. Mrs. Estrom liked to go to bed at precisely ten thirty, and to be woken at seven. Marta found that arrangement usually gave her at least an hour or so to herself, although in this case she was using part of that hour to try to effect repairs to a dripping faucet in the kitchen. Mrs. Estrom could afford to get a plumber in to replace it a thousand times over, but Marta had quickly found that for small things, her employer really didn't see the point of bringing in specialists.

Probably because Mrs. Estrom wasn't the one having to do the work.

There was a *lot* of work when it came to the crumbling old house that had been the Estrom family's home for generations, back since great-great Grandpa Estrom had first made his money on the stock market. It was huge and twisting, big enough that, back in the day, it probably had a small army of staff to maintain it.

These days, there were still staff, but they only came in periodically to do what was needed, and Marta was the one who had to arrange it when they did, making the calls, organizing the schedules. Certainly, when major repairs were needed, Marta had to stand there in her hard hat, overseeing any contractors. The rest of the time, it was just her, seeing to any problems that arose.

1

When she'd taken the job, she'd assumed that she would need to know about schedule management and talking to important people, basic first aid in case Mrs. Estrom's medical conditions got out of hand, and the ability to coordinate with her various business interests, not about the inner workings of butterfly valves or minor electrical repairs.

Which all sounded as if Marta was complaining, but honestly, she found that she loved her job. Mrs. Estrom was about as generous an employer as it was possible to find, and Marta had discovered that she liked knowing that she could take care of all the small things around the place without any problems. Whenever her mother asked why Marta wasn't going off to do something with that business degree that she'd put so much effort into, Marta just pointed out that *this* job paid better than half the low earning positions she'd had trying to get a foot on the ladder in the business world, and probably meant that she would have better connections at the end of it, too.

Marta had just gotten the faucet apart, ready to replace the faulty ceramic cartridge, when she heard the sound of someone moving about the house.

"Mrs. Estrom, is everything ok?"

Her employer didn't usually get up in the night. She slept with an ease and soundness that Marta couldn't help admiring, given that Marta mostly woke up feeling even more tired than she'd been when she went to sleep.

So if she was moving around, maybe there was something wrong. Marta had been trained to deal with a whole range of medical emergencies, since that was a big part of the reason that she was there. Mrs. Estrom's mind might still be as sharp as ever, but at ninety, her body was slowly failing her, one minor medical complaint at a time. If Marta weren't there, she suspected that Mrs. Estrom would quickly find herself in a home of some sort, and as her employer had said, that would kill her quicker than anything else could.

"Mrs. Estrom? Do you need something?" Marta asked as she headed out of the kitchen into the hall. The sounds were coming from the drawing room. Had her employer gotten up in the night because she wanted something from there? Usually, she found it more convenient to call down to Marta in those cases, using the phone she'd given Marta that was *exclusively* for communications between the two of them, so that there was never a chance of someone else being on the line. It meant that Marta sometimes had to get up in the night, just to fetch something from downstairs.

2

Still, Mrs. Estrom was… well, herself, and that meant that she did very much as she pleased. If she wished to wander around her own house at night, that was very much her business, not Marta's. Marta's business was to be there and make sure that everything around her life ran smoothly.

Marta headed for the drawing room. The light was off, so Marta flicked it on, looking around the expensive antique furniture that had been collected over several lifetimes in the family. There was no one there now, but a decanter on a small side table had been knocked over, sending a spill of what Marta knew to be particularly expensive brandy out over the floor.

"Damn it!" Marta said, and hurried forward, trying to find something to clean it up with. Thankfully, she already had a cloth ready, on hand for wiping any excess water from around the faucet. Kneeling, she started to mop it up, imagining what Mrs. Estrom would say when she saw all of this. Would she assume that Marta was drinking on the job? Or had she been the one to cause this? Maybe she was down here somewhere. Maybe she'd had some kind of medical emergency and knocked over the brandy while she staggered off out of the room.

Marta was still worrying about that when she heard the creak of a floorboard behind her. She started to turn, assuming that her employer was in there after all, but a hand grabbed her hair, yanking her head back sharply, forcing her to look up at the ceiling.

Marta cried out as she saw the flash of a knife above her, but it was too late to do anything. She tried to reach out to stop it, but it was already plunging down into her, agony bursting through her as the weapon slid in and out of her as mechanically as a sewing machine.

"Marta, is everything all right dear?" Mrs. Estrom called from upstairs.

Marta didn't have any breath to answer. The knifeman shoved her down to the carpet, and the last thing Marta saw was the sight of her blood mingling with the spilled brandy.

CHAPTER TWO

Paige King barely ducked out of the way of a blow aimed at her head, feeling it pass by just an inch, the whisper of air as it passed scraping across her skin. Another strike came at her, and she lifted her hands to block instinctively, only to find the weight of her attacker barreling into her.

The difference in size was massive, and decisive, impossible to hold back. It meant that she found herself tumbling to the floor, with the bulk of her opponent on top of her. She tried to struggle out from underneath him, the way she'd been shown, but his weight meant that there was no room to execute a simple standup, and her attempts to flip him over to create some room achieved nothing.

Paige saw the moment when her attacker reached back behind him, and she knew without being told what that meant. She'd trained for this.

"Knife!" she called out, reaching to try to control the weapon arm.

Paige wasn't quite quick enough, and she had a moment of absolute terror as the arm came around, the blade a blur as it struck her again and again. Paige felt herself starting to go limp in response to the blows.

"Don't stop!" her instructor yelled from somewhere above her. "Keep fighting!"

Paige did her best, kicking away at her opponent, creating space, but then he was back on top of her, still stabbing.

"Ok, break!"

Paige had rarely been as grateful for anything as she was for those two words. It meant that the large, heavily padded figure of her simulated attacker got off her, while she got to haul herself up off the mats at the FBI academy's training facility.

Around her, other FBI trainees stood waiting for their turn at the side of the mats or working with padded opponents of their own, fighting hard as they tried to keep them at bay. It struck Paige as deeply unfair somehow that all the attackers got to wear massive amounts of padding, while she got none; but she suspected that the unfairness was

4

a deliberate part of the drill. She would have bruises on her ribs from the rubber knife in the morning.

"You have to be more aggressive, King," the instructor said. "You have to take down the suspect, not just wait for him to kill you."

"Yes, sir," Paige said, but honestly, she felt as though that kind of aggression was the one part of this that didn't come easily to her. It was a part of herself she always flinched away from. In the background, she could see other students elbowing and punching, lashing out with everything they had. She wasn't sure if she really had that in her.

"Ok, back to the line. And when it's your turn again, I want to see you be more proactive about all this."

Paige went back to the side, standing among all the other FBI trainees in their sweatpants and FBI t-shirts. Paige had never worn a uniform before, had never even been in the Girl Scouts, and it felt strange to be just one more almost identical part of a big machine.

She wondered what anyone from college would think if they could see her now, red hair slick with sweat, youthful features flushed with the effort of training so hard. Probably, they would ask her exactly why she'd completed her PhD in criminal psychology, looking at one of the nation's worst serial killers, only to jump straight into training to be an FBI agent after helping to recapture him when he escaped, rather than going into the more sedate world of academia as she'd been preparing to do.

Paige might not have been able to give a coherent answer to that just a few months ago when she'd signed up for the FBI academy in the wake of helping to catch escaped serial killer Adam Riker. She may have said something general about how it would let her put the things she'd learned to practical use, rather than being sat in an academic office, reading dusty books. Slowly, that had crystalized into the feeling that this was where Paige was meant to be, what she was meant to be doing.

Although it was kind of hard to maintain that feeling when she'd just been stabbed repeatedly with a rubber knife, hard enough to leave bruises.

"Higgs is a hard-ass," another of the trainees there, a young Hispanic woman named Rosa, said. She was taller than Paige, and obviously in shape. She excelled in the physical aspects of the training in a way that Paige simply didn't. "Hang in there. You'll be fine."

It was her turn next, and Rosa went out hard, slamming into the opponent in the padded suit, giving him no time to get to the knife before she had him pinned to the floor, wrenching him over onto his stomach into an arrest position and controlling him there until the instructor called a halt.

Paige wished that she could do that kind of thing so easily. So far in the training, all the didactic aspects had been fine for her, memorizing the law and procedures she needed to know, how to maintain the chain of evidence, how to go about reading a crime scene. Paige had been a natural when it came to interrogation technique, and when they'd gone through classic cases in their sessions to understand how the FBI had gone about solving them, Paige had already known most of them. She was *good* at that kind of thing.

The physical aspects were harder, though. Paige was just about keeping up when it came to the running and the physical fitness, but she barely made it around the obstacle courses, and hand to hand combat like this was harder still. She could hit the target with a pistol, but that got a lot harder when they did drills designed to simulate an actual situation. Paige found herself, every time, thinking back to the moment when she'd shot Adam Riker in order to try to save her mother. The result was a lack of aggression that meant failing, over and over.

Paige hoped that she was getting better, slowly learning what she would need to be an agent, and then how to apply it as a profiler once she made it into the FBI. In spite of the difficulty of the physical aspects of the course, she was determined to keep going, whatever it took.

"King, you're up again!" Higgs called out.

Paige steeled herself, going forward, squaring up to her heavily padded foe. Whatever it took, she reminded herself, as that foe surged forward.

*

Paige groaned and iced the worst of her bruises in her room at the training facility. That last session had hurt, but there was no slacking off from the next training session. That would just be an admission that she wasn't up to the demands of being an agent, of going out into the world and catching bad guys. She had to grit her teeth and keep going.

She sat there, reading through another book on investigative technique while she waited for the pain in her ribs to subside. Paige couldn't concentrate, though, and in any case, she'd already made notes on this chapter once. Throughout the training, Paige had always applied all the techniques she'd used in her research to the process of learning, forcing the information into her head so that it would be there again whenever she needed it in the future.

Honestly, compared to the process of trying to write a PhD, the intellectual part of this was easy. Most things were, it turned out. It had been easy for Paige to forget when she'd been doing her PhD that she was actually good at this kind of thing. A PhD was designed to challenge people who were already pretty much at the top of their class, and while she'd been doing hers, the only other students Paige had spent much time around had also been grad students. Researching at a high level had just seemed… well, normal.

Paige was still working on the finer theoretical points of how the FBI went about tailing someone, using multiple teams handing over to one another, when her mother called. There had been times in the past when Paige might not have picked up immediately, worried about the way the conversation would go, when she would have had to build herself up to the prospect of talking to her mother.

Now though, Paige picked up straight away. Almost losing her mother those few months back, when Adam Riker had kidnapped her and tried to get Paige to kill her, had been a kind of catalyst for the two of them to start talking again. Paige had even been down to Virginia a couple of times to see her, before she'd enrolled with the FBI.

"Hey Mom," Paige said, sitting back on her neatly made bed. "Is everything ok over there? Are *you* ok?"

That had been one of Paige's biggest worries in the last few months: that the brush with death would leave a mark on her mother that she wouldn't be able to shake. An event like that had to inspire some level of PTSD, didn't it? That moment, that whole attempt to find Adam after he escaped from a secure psychiatric institution, had certainly left its marks on Paige. She saw his victims in her dreams at night, along with the moment that she'd shot him.

"I'm fine," her mother said.

"Are you sure?" Paige asked. Her mother was the kind of person who would probably say that things were fine even when they were anything but that. It was something she'd definitely done when Paige was a kid, first not talking about her father's death at the hands of a serial killer, and then about the abuse that Paige had suffered at the hands of her stepfather, as if ignoring it would make it all go away.

7

Paige realized now that not talking had been her mother's way of trying to cope with things. The only problem with that was that Paige had needed to talk about it almost as much as her mother had needed not to. It had left Paige feeling as if her mother didn't care, had left her resentful and only too eager to get away from home when the time had come to go to college.

Yet, when Adam had tried to tell her how much she hated her mother, when he'd told her to shoot her mother, she'd realized that she didn't feel that kind of resentment. She didn't hate her mother, didn't blame her for what had happened. Paige loved her. None of it had been her mother's fault, and she'd done everything she could to keep Paige safe.

"I'm sure," her mother said. "Things have been going… actually, pretty well. Did I tell you that I got a promotion at my job?"

"No," Paige said.

"Well, not really a promotion, more that Mr. Phelps, my boss, just wants me to take on a few extra responsibilities. Of course, that means that I've had to cut back on my Tuesday book club a bit, but the extra money comes in handy, and I still see most of the girls for drinks on the weekend. Sandy has a new man in her life, and Emma…"

Paige let the flood of small talk about life in an even smaller town wash over her, grateful to hear about a life that was just *normal* compared to hers. It wasn't a life she could live, but she was glad that it was a life her mother got to be happy with. She was glad that her mother got to have a life without violence, after everything that had happened.

"What about you?" her mother asked after a little while. "How are things going over at the FBI?"

Paige tried to decide how much to tell her mother. "The training is tough," Paige said, "but I'm hanging in there. I can handle it."

"I still can't quite believe that's where you decided you wanted to go next with your life," her mother said. "I thought when you finished your PhD you might be done with killers and criminals, but now you're going to be actively chasing them."

That was one thing that didn't seem to have changed. Her mother still didn't quite seem to get how important it was for Paige to understand more about the criminal mind. Possibly, she would never quite get it. After all, her mother's response to her husband's death had been to run away from it as hard as she could.

"It's what I want to do, Mom. It's where I can make a difference."

"But you'll be in danger in the FBI."

"I can handle the danger, Mom," Paige said. She hoped that it was true.

Paige found her conversation interrupted by a knock at the door of her room.

"Sorry, Mom, I have to go. Someone's here to see me."

"Ok, Paige. Stay safe. I hope I'll see you soon. I love you."

"I love you too, Mom."

Paige hung up and then hurried over to the door. She was surprised to see one of the other people there in the course outside, a young man with a buzz cut and built like a linebacker, looking at her with a serious expression.

"Paige King? You are to report to the administrator's office at once." Something about his tone made it sound both serious and urgent, and that tone worried Paige.

She frowned at the demand. "What's this about?"

"I wasn't told. Only that you have to come *now*."

Paige nodded. If she was going to join the FBI, she had to get used to following orders. "All right. I'm on my way."

Paige started to make her way through the training facility, heading down through the dorm that held the prospective agents and then out into a broad courtyard that had other dorm blocks on three sides. Behind them were the training buildings and classrooms used to prepare her and the others for their potential future jobs as FBI agents. There were whole replica houses there to practice close quarter battle and breaches in hostage situations, a track designed to teach defensive driving, and a gun range.

Paige didn't make her way towards any of those, however, but instead headed for the small administrative building near the front of the campus. It was old with large windows and ivy growing up the walls, an almost Victorian look to the architecture. As she walked, she tried to work out what this was about, and the more Paige thought about it, the more the walk filled her with a sense of impending dread.

Previously, the only people she'd seen summoned in this way had been people who hadn't been making the cut, or who had managed to break the rules. They'd been called there to be told that they were being let go from the program, and that their things would be waiting by the gate. There weren't a lot of second chances when the program was meant to turn out people who could protect the public and catch bad guys.

Was that about to happen to her, even after all the effort that she'd put in? Was she doing that badly in the more physical aspects of all of this that it canceled out her good work everywhere else?

The prospect of it made Paige feel sick even as she kept walking to the admin building. She couldn't just not go. She'd been sent for. It wasn't as if she had a choice.

Paige stepped inside and went up to the receptionist at the front desk.

"Yes?"

"Paige King," she said.

"Ah, yes." Even the receptionist sounded as if she didn't approve of Paige being there. "Second floor. Conference room A."

Was that where they told people that they were being cut? There was no clue in the name, and Paige had to make her way up a set of stairs almost trembling at the prospect. She looked around until she found a large set of double doors labeled as the conference room, then knocked.

"Come in."

Paige stepped inside. There were two figures in there already, at one end of a long oval conference desk. One, she knew vaguely by sight as former agent Tom Podovski, the administrative head here, a man in his sixties, with steel gray hair, lined features, and an overweight frame.

The other, she knew much better than that. Agent Christopher Marriott stood as Paige entered, letting her take in his solid, six-foot-four body, his sandy hair, his square jaw and almost boyish good looks. Paige couldn't help staring. What was *he* doing here?

"Paige, there you are," he said. "Please, sit down. I need your help."

CHAPTER THREE

Paige sat down opposite Christopher, feeling both glad to see him and relieved that this almost certainly wouldn't be about cutting her from the FBI academy. They didn't have to call in full FBI agents to do that, after all. This was something else. The only question now was what.

She looked around the conference room, at the screens set there and the large, leather-backed chairs. All of this for her? Whatever this was, it had to be something important. Why was Christopher here, though? Paige could see a file set on the table. Was it to do with her?

"It's good to see you," Paige said, and it was; it really was. A part of her had hoped that the intervening months would have done something to dull the way her body reacted every time she saw him, the attraction that was always there under the surface. Not for the first time, she had to remind herself that Christopher had a wife.

They'd kept in touch a little, after everything that had happened with Adam Riker, but all of that had been polite and professional, certainly on Christopher's side. Paige had forced herself to do the same, knowing that it wouldn't be right to do anything else.

"You too, Paige," he said. "I was glad to hear you actually did it and enrolled at the academy."

"Ms. King here is acing the more academic components of the course," the administrative head said. "Once we get her up to speed on the more physical aspects of the job, I'm sure that she'll be a fine agent."

He looked across to Christopher, and there was a message in that look that Paige couldn't decipher. It seemed obvious to her that they'd been having some kind of conversation about her before she came in, and that this was a continuation of it, but she didn't have enough details to work out more. She was more worried about the implied rebuke of the administrative head's words. She really needed to get better at the physical side of becoming an agent.

"Unfortunately, I can't wait that long," Christopher replied, in a tone that made it clear that this had been settled before Paige walked into the room.

"What's going on here?" Paige asked. "I'm pretty sure that this isn't a social call, or I wouldn't have been summoned to the administration building."

Christopher looked suddenly serious, as if remembering the real reason for his visit.

"You're right. I wish I could say that this was just because I wanted to check up on how you're doing, but I'm here because of what you can do, Paige."

He pushed the file across the table towards her, his hand just brushing hers as Paige took it.

"What's this?" Paige asked. Before, she'd assumed that it was a file on her. Now, though, Christopher had caught her interest.

Paige opened the file and found herself looking at a picture of a young woman.

"That is Marta Huarez, personal assistant and caretaker to Mrs. Eugenie Estrom. Marta was murdered last night in her employer's house, taken by surprise and stabbed repeatedly."

Paige frowned at that, a spark of memory flickering within her at the mention of the word 'caretaker.' She thought then that she understood what all of this was about, except that it couldn't be, could it?

"Wait, you aren't talking about-"

"Lars Ingram."

He dropped those words into the conversation like lead weights. They certainly made Paige stare at the file in front of her more intently. She saw more pictures of the crime scene, with the body face down on bloodstained carpets, evidence markers pointing out the blood spatters but very little else.

"The caretaker killer?" Paige said. She'd studied his work, the way she'd studied that of so many other serial killers. But there was an obvious problem with the idea that it might be Lars Ingram. "But they *caught* him."

"Caught, tried, and sentenced," Christopher agreed. "He's currently on death row awaiting his imminent execution after being convicted of nine counts of murder. From your expression, I guess you remember the details?"

Paige saw the academy's administrative head looking at her as if waiting to be impressed by his star student. Christopher gave her a similar look. It was obvious that this was about making some kind of

12

point to Agent Podovski. Paige nodded. She could definitely remember the details.

"Nine murders that were identified as his, starting maybe three or four years ago, all of women aged 18 to 30, all engaged in taking care of someone. Overnight caretakers, au pairs, family members looking after a dying relative. All of them stabbed seven times and left to die in places that should have been secure."

She checked the file, looking for the coroner's report.

"Yes," Christopher said. "Marta Huarez was stabbed seven times, the same as all the others. So was another young woman two days ago."

And *that* was impossible. Paige had read through the case, and the evidence against Ingram was conclusive. After a tip off, DNA that had been found at his last crime scene was linked to him, and he'd barely even bothered to conceal what he'd done when he was caught. He'd been *proud* of it. This wasn't a case of mistaken identity, with the real killer still out there somewhere. The jury had no difficulty at all in convicting him, or in recommending the death sentence.

He'd entered a plea of insanity, of course, or at least, his lawyers had done it on his behalf. From what Paige understood of the case, Ingram hadn't liked that. Psychopaths sometimes didn't. Their condition made them feel like gods, superior to other people, not mentally ill. They sometimes thought that they were the only ones who were truly sane.

The plea hadn't worked, in any case. Psychopath or not, Ingram had been deemed responsible for his crimes. Now Ingram was waiting for execution.

"So it's some kind of copycat?" Paige said. That was the only plausible explanation.

"That appears to be the case," Christopher agreed. "The details are too close for the similarities just to be a coincidence."

Paige sat there, staring at the file for several more seconds. There were detailed descriptions of the probable blade used, some kind of hunting knife, along with descriptions of each injury, the time of death, and the surrounding scene. It appeared that a decanter of brandy had been knocked over, and the file suggested that might have been during the struggle.

"This file is wrong," Paige said.

"I'm sure the coroner did a thorough job, Ms. King," Administrator Podovski said.

Paige shook her head, though. She was sure about this part.

"What do you see, Paige?" Christopher asked.

"The decanter that was knocked over, the file suggests it might indicate a struggle, but the coroner's report shows no defensive wounds. More than that, though, the other cases by Ingram show us why it was knocked over."

Christopher looked intrigued at that, and Paige found herself playing up to that expression. She wanted to impress him. She felt as if she'd been called there *specifically* to impress.

"Why is that?" he asked.

"With Ingram's other victims, every one of them was ambushed in their own home, or the home of their employer. They were lured to a particular spot where Ingram was waiting, using some kind of distraction. My guess is that the brandy was the distraction in this case. It's another element the copycat has copied."

"That makes a lot of sense," Christopher said. "You know the previous cases well?"

"I've read them," Paige said, not wanting to make too much of it. "It's not like I could take a spot test on all of them, or anything."

She didn't want to pretend that she was an expert on this case, when she'd come across the details only in passing. The academic work on these murders had been useful, though, in deciding on the directions she was going to go with her own work for her PhD. While the world of true crime writing was broad, the truly academic side of it was smaller.

She saw Christopher looking over at Administrator Podovski.

"You see my point?"

"Impressive, of course," the administrator said. "But the fact remains that she has not completed her training."

Paige cleared her throat, pointedly. She was getting tired of being talked about with no idea of what was happening.

"Could someone please explain to me exactly what's going on? What am I doing here? What are *you* doing here, Christopher, if you're on this case? Shouldn't you be off looking for the killer?"

She saw Christopher shrug. "I will be, just as soon as I have the kind of backup that I need to actually find this guy and bring him to justice."

Paige ran those words through her head a few times, the meaning slowly sinking in. Backup?

"Wait, you mean me?" she said, caught by surprise even now, simply because it seemed impossible that she could be asked when she wasn't fully trained yet. She realized that this was the reason she'd been summoned to the administration building. This was the reason Christopher wanted to see her face to face after so long.

"Yes, you," Christopher replied. "I think that you understand serial killers better than anyone I've met, and I've seen firsthand how useful your instincts can be in a case like this one."

"But I'm not even fully trained yet," Paige insisted. She might be training to be an agent, but she wasn't one yet, and her instructors were clear that she still had a way to go before she was done. Even after she completed her training, there would still be a period of probation, and of working her way up through the ranks. If she wanted to achieve her aim of becoming a profiler, then she would need to wait for an opening in the BAU, apply, and go through an additional selection process. She couldn't just walk out of her training to jump onto a case.

"That's what I've been trying to tell the agent," Administrator Podovski said. He sounded as if he didn't entirely approve of any of this. It clearly wasn't the way things were meant to be done, and Paige got the feeling that the administrator was a man who liked things to be done according to the rules. "You show great promise, Paige, but we can't just throw you into a dangerous situation when you're not ready."

"And what I've been telling you," Christopher shot back, "is that this murderer isn't going to wait until Paige is fully qualified. The situation is too urgent. I need her help, and I need it now."

That still didn't make complete sense to Paige. Christopher had the full resources of the FBI behind him, after all.

"Why me?" Paige asked.

"I told you, I need the backup, and-"

"Yes, but why *me*?" Paige asked. "You have the BAU behind you. They have plenty of fully trained profilers working for them. You could have gone to any one of them, and they would help you with this. So why me, Agent Marriott? What is there about me that makes you want me working with you rather than one of them?"

That was the key question here. Why did Christopher want her on this case, rather than one of the fully trained professionals he had available to him? What was it about Paige that had made him think of her?

"I've worked with them, and I've worked with you, Paige," he said. "I honestly trust your instincts more than I trust those of any of the profilers working at the BAU. And things are happening too quickly. I know how you'll react under pressure. I know that if anyone can work this out, it's you. Yes, I could get another profiler, but I don't want that. I want the best, and I honestly believe that's you.

Paige felt slightly embarrassed at that kind of praise, but also strangely proud. She *wanted* to prove to Christopher that she could do this, that she could live up to everything that he thought of her. She wanted to show him that she could be everything that he needed her to be.

"But I'm in the middle of my training," Paige tried. "I'm not sure I would even be allowed to leave to do something like this."

Administrator Podovski cleared his throat. "Agent Marriott and I have already had this discussion. The academy accepts that catching a killer is the most important thing. We are prepared to release you from your studies on a temporary basis. You would have to make that training up, though."

Paige nodded; she could do that.

"And you will have to remember that you are *not* yet an agent," Administrator Podovski said. "You do not have the power to arrest people. You will not be carrying a weapon. I will not have a situation where a trainee is running around the streets, shooting people."

Paige was fine with that. Those parts of the curriculum were the ones that she had the biggest problems with anyway. She would leave that side of things to Christopher if it came to it, although she suspected that he would want her close by, whatever they did.

"What do you say, Paige?" Christopher asked. "I can't force you to do this. You're not a trained agent yet, so I can't go around giving you orders, but I really need your help on this. I think with you and me, we have a real chance to catch this guy."

When he put it like that, Paige knew that she *didn't* have a choice, not really. She couldn't just stand by if other women might be killed. She found herself nodding.

"All right," she said. "I'm in. Where do we start?"

"At the murder scene."

CHAPTER FOUR

Paige had to admit that she was impressed by the Estrom family home. It was huge, pretty much a mansion, and had obviously sat there for at least a hundred years or so on the same spot. It looked as if it had been built and rebuilt over that period, worked on by generation after generation of the same family, each member wanting to put their own stamp on the place.

It stood at the heart of extensive gardens, mostly lawns but with a large rose garden around to the side. Its nearest neighbors were far enough away that even calling them neighbors seemed like the wrong word to use. Paige seriously doubted that this was the kind of place where people just came over to check on one another or to speak to the occupants of the houses nearby.

Under normal circumstances, it would have been a quiet place, just far out enough from the main body of D.C. that it would have brought peace, while still being close enough to the city for easy access. The kind of place that probably had diplomats and officials living in some of the surrounding buildings.

Today, though, there was nothing peaceful about it. Police vehicles littered the driveway leading up to it, some with their lights still flashing. Paige could see a uniformed officer at the door, while around the edges of the property, reporters stood with cameras, their broadcast vans parked nearby, all obviously hungry for a story.

For a moment or two, Paige might have been back at one of the crime scenes around the women Adam Riker had murdered. She still had memories of having to push through crowds of reporters, while they called out questions that were far too personal for her. That brought feelings of worry bubbling to the surface within Paige. What if she couldn't do this?

"Are you ok?" Christopher asked.

He'd noticed her discomfort, which suggested that he was watching her at least some of the time as he drove. Paige didn't know what to feel about that. A part of her wanted him to watch her, wanted him to be interested in her, because he was an intelligent, kind, dynamic guy. Every time she thought that, though, Paige found herself thinking of

Justine, his wife, reminding herself that she couldn't be interested in him, and he definitely wasn't interested in her.

"I'm fine," Paige said, trying not to make too much of it. "I'm just remembering the last crime scene we were at."

Christopher gave her a serious look then as they pulled up in front of the house.

"Can you do this, Paige? If you don't think that you're going to be able to handle this, I can take you back. I know you're not trained yet. Maybe I'm asking too much."

Paige tried to look as determined as possible. "I have to be able to do this kind of thing if I'm going to be an agent. I'm pretty sure that it's not optional whether I look at crime scenes once I make it into the Bureau."

And if word got back that she hadn't been able to bring herself to look at another body, then Paige was pretty sure that would be it as far as her chances of joining the FBI were concerned. It needed people who could do the job, not ones who needed to be babysat through every part of it.

"That might be true," Christopher said, "but that's not what I asked. Can you do this, Paige?"

"I can do this," Paige assured him, hoping that it was true as she said it. It had to be true. She would *make* it true.

They got out of the car and headed to the house. Christopher held up his ID and the cop at the door stood aside to let them pass. There were crime scene investigators working their way through the house, testing almost every available surface, and for a moment or two Paige was worried about the possibility that she and Christopher were contaminating the crime scene; but with both of their prints and DNA on file, she guessed that it didn't matter so much, especially when the techs had last night to go through the place. Even so, both of them pulled on gloves as they moved into the crime scene.

"Anything?" Christopher asked one of the techs, a young man who looked to Paige as if he should still have been in school rather than working his way through a crime scene wearing a plastic evidence suit.

"Nothing so far," he replied. "Whoever did this was careful enough not to leave anything behind."

Which matched what Paige knew of Lars Ingram's crimes. Until he'd slipped up with his last murder, he'd been precise about cleaning up after himself. He'd been almost clinical as he broke in, not leaving

18

any trace. There had been an almost total contrast between that caution and the savagery of the attacks.

"This way," Christopher said, leading Paige through to a drawing room that was tastefully decorated with antique furniture, with expensive oil paintings sitting on the walls, and a row of books that looked as though they'd been bought by the yard finishing the effect that great wealth had been accumulating for some considerable time. It was much more opulent than anything Paige had been around for most of her life.

It occurred to Paige that, if Christopher was leading her through this place so easily, he must have been there before he came to find her. He must have taken a look at this crime scene and only then decided that he needed her help. That was both gratifying and slightly worrying, because it meant a lot of pressure on Paige's shoulders to find an answer for him.

Still, she was there to do a job, and she was determined to do it well.

"This is where the murder happened," Christopher said.

Paige could see the blood stains on the carpet where Marta Huarez had been killed, marking the spot as surely as if the body had still been there. She could see the decanter lying empty on the floor, and the straight line from there to the door. She guessed that the killer would have hidden behind that door before he leapt out to kill her. It was a simple ambush, but effective when Marta Huarez had no reason to suspect that there was any danger.

Christopher led her over to a window. "The latch on this window was forced. The house is old enough that there aren't locks on all the windows, so the killer was able to use that to get inside. There are partial footprints in the flowerbeds outside the window, but nothing that seems specific."

Paige guessed that he'd gotten all of this from the techs around the scene, and there were definitely plenty of them. They would be the ones running down scraps of evidence, which meant that *her* job was more about working out what the killer wanted, and why he was there, trying to help Christopher in any way that she could.

"The owner of the house didn't hear anything?" Paige asked.

Christopher gestured to the door. "You can ask her yourself. I want to hear what you make of her. Come on."

He led the way through the house, to a large dining room where an older woman was sitting on a dining chair, being looked over by someone who appeared to be a doctor. The woman was wrinkled and white haired, wearing a severe dark dress and a set of pearls. A cane rested against the chair that she sat in, her crabbed right hand sitting on top of its handle, clutching it tightly every few seconds. She seemed distraught, but as she looked Paige's way, her eyes were sharp and alive with intelligence.

"I think that will have to be enough for now, Henry," she told the doctor. "I believe the FBI have more questions for me."

The doctor straightened up from his examination. He was a middle aged, balding man in a dark suit. Paige could see the slight sheen of sweat on his brow that came from worry.

"You're not to stress Mrs. Estrom any further than she already has been," he said, in a tone that didn't allow for any argument. "At ninety years old, her health is *quite* delicate enough without all of this."

"We'll be as brief as we can be," Paige assured him. She had no wish to make today any worse for the older woman if she could avoid it. At the same time, though, there were things she needed to know.

She looked over to Christopher, who took the lead.

"Mrs. Estrom?" he said, stepping in front of the older woman. "My name is Agent Marriott. This is my associate, Paige King. I was hoping to go through things with you again, if that's all right."

Paige saw Mrs. Estrom nod, although she could also see the strain in her eyes. Paige guessed that it had to be difficult for her to go over and over all of this. Each time would be like reliving it.

"Can you tell us what you remember about last night?" Christopher asked.

The older woman hesitated for several seconds, her hand gripping her cane tighter. When she spoke, it was obvious that she was forcing the words out.

"There isn't much to tell," she said. "I normally go to sleep around half past ten at night. I woke up last night because I heard something."

"What kind of something?" Paige asked.

"I don't know," Mrs. Estrom replied. "I *think* it was the sound of something being knocked over, or maybe it was the window. It's hard to say. The next thing I heard was…" she trailed off for a moment or two, and Paige could see tears in her eyes. "I heard Marta scream. I heard her scream, and there was nothing I could do to help her. I called for the police, and I tried to help, but it took me forever to get down the stairs. That's when I found…"

This time, she didn't complete the sentence. She didn't need to, because Paige could guess what she'd found. Her personal assistant lying dead in the drawing room. Paige had seen the photographs in the file Christopher had shown her, and she knew better than anyone the effect of seeing something like that on a person. She'd been the one to find her father after he'd been murdered, after all.

"Did you see anything that seemed out of place when you came downstairs?" Paige asked. "Anything that was where it shouldn't be, or that seemed strange to you?"

Mrs. Estrom shook her head, though, sharply, as if trying to dismiss the image from her mind.

"When you saw Marta's body," she asked, "was she missing anything? Any small items of jewelry or personal possessions?"

Lars Ingram hadn't taken trophies, but perhaps whoever had done this wanted something. It was a different killer, after all, and perhaps something like that might lead back to him.

"No, nothing like that."

"How long had Marta worked for you?" Paige asked.

"Perhaps two years. Ever since my family gave me an ultimatum. I could get live in help, or I could move to a retirement home." There was a note of anger in her voice at the thought of it that made it clear exactly what she thought of that suggestion. "Marta is… was so good to me. She was there for all the medical things, of course, but she also helped out so much around here. She never made a fuss, and she was always so cheerful about her job."

Paige had the feeling that this counted as high praise from the older woman, of a kind that she wouldn't normally give to most people.

"Did she ever talk about having any enemies?" Christopher asked. Paige understood that it was a question that he had to ask. While this looked like the work of Lars Ingram, since they knew it couldn't be him, maybe someone was using his MO as a way to disguise their crime. Maybe someone who knew Marta more personally and had an equally personal reason to want her dead.

Paige didn't think it was that, though, not if another young woman had been killed the same way just a couple of days ago, but she also knew that Christopher had to check.

"No, nothing like that," Mrs. Estrom said. "I can't imagine her having enemies. People always liked Marta so much. I found that I relied on her more and more for that kind of thing, dealing with people. Oh, what am I going to do now?"

"What *are* you going to do now?" Paige asked. "Will you go somewhere else? Perhaps stay with your family for a while until all of this is sorted out?"

She saw the older woman shake her head, though. "And leave this house? No, whatever has happened here, this is still my home. They'll have to carry me out."

There was a level of determination there that Paige guessed wouldn't be talked down by any doctors or family members. Not that there were any members of Mrs. Estrom's family there. She imagined that had to be lonely, being in a house this size with only one assistant for company. And now she'd had to listen to that assistant being murdered while she was helpless upstairs, unable to do anything to help.

Paige imagined that had to be horrifying for her and wished that she could do something to help. She had to remind herself that she *was* trying to help. She was trying to catch the man who'd done this and give Marta justice for her murder.

Paige could see that the older woman was getting pretty stressed now, and out of the corner of her eye, she could see the doctor starting to edge closer again, obviously ready to move her and Christopher on.

"Thank you for your time, Mrs. Estrom," Christopher said, gesturing to Paige that they should back away.

She nodded and stepped back. They'd obviously learned everything they were going to get from Marta's former employer. The old woman hadn't been in a position to see more.

What they'd gotten didn't amount to much. They'd confirmed the time the murder had taken place, and that Mrs. Estrom had heard but not seen it. They hadn't found some obvious piece of evidence to point to a killer, and it seemed that Marta didn't have any enemies.

They weren't going to get a conclusion to this case that easily. Paige just hoped that there would be more when they looked at the other murder, the one that had taken place a couple of days ago.

CHAPTER FIVE

Christopher knew that they needed to find another way to make progress, and quickly. The killer was still out there somewhere.

He was more than glad that he'd been able to persuade Paige to help with this. Yes, he could have gotten one of the profilers from the BAU to do the work, but after everything she'd done on the Adam Riker case, the fact was that Christopher trusted Paige more than all of them.

"Tell me about the other case," Paige said as they left Mrs. Estrom's home. "The one from a couple of days ago."

There was a confidence now when it came to these things that hadn't been there when they'd been trying to recapture Adam Riker. Was that the result of the FBI training she was undertaking, or was it just that she felt more able to speak out now that she was no longer being targeted by a serial killer?

Either way, it was good, and Christopher was more than happy to fill her in.

"I have a copy of that file in the car," he said. "I'll explain it all there."

He led the way back to his dark sedan, and on looking at the surrounding press corps, he drove them a little way away before he pulled over and got out the file for Paige to look at. He didn't want them to have a chance to take a picture of it with a long lens.

"Zoe Wells," Christopher said, giving her the basics as Paige read. "Twenty-seven. Working as an overnight nurse at the Cherry Blossom Retirement Home. An intruder broke in during the night, stabbed her seven times, and then left her for the residents to find in the morning."

He could see Paige reading, absorbing the information with an intensity that Christopher couldn't hope to match, and wondered what she was seeing as she did so. Christopher felt certain that the two of them looked at files in two different ways, with him coming from the point of view of an agent looking for small strands of evidence to follow, and her trying more to get to the heart of what the people involved wanted and thought. It was useful to have that other point of view on all of this, and Christopher hoped that it would be enough to allow the two of them to find the killer between them.

"Do we know how the killer got inside?" Paige asked, after a minute or two of reading.

"The doors have a key code lock to let guests in and out. We think the killer found out that code somehow and used it to get inside. It wasn't exactly a well-guarded secret. It was less to protect the residents and more to prevent those residents with dementia from wandering out of the home."

Paige winced slightly at that.

"What is it?" Christopher asked.

"Just the thought of how poorly protected they all were."

"No one thought that there would be a killer coming for them," Christopher pointed out. That was one thing that was important to remember in this job, that while they saw death and violence on an almost daily basis, ordinary people didn't. Of course, before Paige had signed up for the FBI academy, she'd already been working with the worst kind of killers, and had seen her own father murdered when she was a teenager.

"But one came anyway," Paige said. "Did he lure this victim into position the same way he did with Marta Huarez?"

"We think so," Christopher said. "One of the personal alarms some of the residents wear was activated and found on the floor of the room where she had been killed."

"So he made her think that one of the people in the home was in trouble and then killed her when she went to help?"

Christopher saw the look of disgust that crossed Paige's face at that, and he found himself hoping that she would be able to keep this professional. He needed someone who could look at this objectively. Or did he? One of Paige's strengths was the way that she could get into people's heads.

"We'll go and take a look there, try to speak to Ms. Wells's colleagues," Christopher said. "I talked to them yesterday, but if we're lucky, they'll have remembered something that might help us to make some progress on this."

He saw Paige nod as he put the car into gear.

"There's no mention of camera footage in the file," Paige said. "In a retirement home, wouldn't there be cameras to try to ensure that the residents are safe?"

"There were a couple," Christopher said. "But it was a long way from total coverage. We're going through the footage, but it looks as if the killer was able to avoid them."

"Does that mean that he scouted it beforehand?" Paige asked.

It was a good question. Someone managing to avoid all of the cameras in a building suggested that they knew where those cameras were ahead of time. Doing that in some buildings might mean access to plans of the layout, but somewhere like this, it probably meant watching the location until he was sure.

"The trouble is that it would be easy for them to do so," Christopher said. "There are a lot of agency staff, and a lot of visitors. And that's assuming that they even did case the retirement home before they struck."

While it was likely, it wasn't certain. Someone used to breaking into locations might have the expertise to avoid cameras without that kind of preparation.

"I'm going to have a tech check the footage," Christopher said. "That's not the reason I have you here."

"You want me to try to get into the killer's head," Paige said.

Christopher nodded. The more they could understand about the killer, the better the chance that they might be able to catch him before he killed anyone else.

For now, though, they needed to talk to people at the Cherry Blossom Retirement Home. Christopher pulled his car up outside it, the home a sprawling, modern building that had been made to look a little less imposing by honeysuckle climbing up the side and a few trees out front.

There wasn't the same spread of police vehicles that there had been at the Estrom house. Those had already been and gone, the crime scene investigators having done their work. Even the reporters had moved on to the new killing. It meant that everything was quiet as Christopher and Paige got out and headed over to the front door.

They were met by a male orderly who wore medical scrubs and had a lanyard around his neck that identified him as Billy. He was a large man, but there was a soft edge to him, only added to by the apologetic smile he gave Paige and Christopher.

"I'm sorry," he said. "We sent out an email to the families of the residents the other day. There has been an incident here, and for a couple of days we've been advised to keep visitors away."

Christopher held up his ID.

25

"We're not visiting relatives," he said. "We're here to talk to the staff and residents about the murder."

Christopher saw the change in the man's expression. It was more worried now, obviously unsettled by the presence of himself and Paige. He waved them inside, into a hallway lined with comfortable chairs and artwork that was obviously designed to be used for a waiting area.

"We've only just managed to calm some of the residents down after what happened," Billy said. "Mr. Graves, the man who found poor Zoe, had to be sedated."

"Would it be possible to talk to him about what he saw?" Paige asked.

The orderly shook his head almost instantly. "It won't do you any good. He has Alzheimer's. Even when he started calling for help, I didn't think there was anything seriously wrong. He can react that way sometimes. You just have to distract him and let him talk until he calms down a little."

That was what they'd said the last time Christopher had been here. And he doubted that anything would have improved with time. Even Paige couldn't get anything out of a man who literally couldn't remember.

"And it would put a lot of additional stress on him," the orderly replied, obviously trying to protect the resident.

Christopher was willing to let that go. He wasn't about to make life worse for one old man, especially when there was no prospect of getting useful information from him.

"You were here, though," Paige said. "You said that you heard him calling for help. What did *you* see?"

Christopher was impressed that she'd caught that.

"I saw… I saw Zoe just lying there, face down. I saw the blood. I tried to help her, but there was Mr. Graves screaming, and other residents coming around to look, and… it was just chaos. People everywhere."

Meaning that the CSI team probably wouldn't have any usable DNA or fingerprint results for them. The whole scene would be far too contaminated for that, even if the killer hadn't been as careful as he seemed to have been at the Estrom house.

"Were you here the night before?" Paige asked.

Billy nodded at that. "I sleep here a lot of nights. In a place like this, you want more than one overnight nurse on duty, because if anything happens, you need the extra pair of hands to be able to move people, or to deal with one thing while another happens."

"And did you see or hear anything out of the ordinary?" Paige asked.

To Christopher, the orderly looked almost guilty as Paige said that. Was he hiding something?

"No, I didn't," Billy said. "And if I had, maybe Zoe would still be alive. If I'd seen this guy coming in…"

"Then it might have been you dead," Christopher said. "You couldn't do anything to protect her."

That was what the guilt was: not being able to save someone he'd worked with. Guilt at not being able to help. Christopher saw that from witnesses sometimes. They thought that they'd failed the victim because they hadn't managed to see something that would allow the perpetrator to be captured immediately. He'd seen it from agents too, even felt it, knowing that every delay on a case might allow a killer to kill again.

"Can you tell us about Zoe?" Paige asked. "What was she like?"

"She was always so bright and vivacious," Billy said. "So good with the residents. Always there to help when they needed her."

"Do you know much about her life outside of here?" Paige asked.

"She had a pretty quiet life, I think," Billy said. "Lived alone in a rental apartment, saving up for a deposit to actually buy somewhere. She used to talk about how one day she was going to move to the West Coast somewhere."

"Did anyone dislike her?" Christopher asked, wanting to know if there was anywhere obvious that they could start to look for answers.

Billy looked genuinely perplexed by the question. "How could anyone dislike Zoe? She was great. Is that what you think this is? Someone she upset? But she never hurt anyone."

"We just have to look into every possibility," Paige said. "We won't take up any more of your time, although I imagine Agent Marriott will want to talk to your manager and make sure that there's nothing on Zoe's records that might help us."

Christopher wanted exactly that, but he also suspected Paige had said it mostly as a way to bring the conversation to a close.

"Sure, it's just down there," Billy said, pointing.

"I don't think there's anything here," Paige said, as the two of them started to walk. "We're going around asking all the questions we'd ask with a normal murder, but I don't think that's going to do us any good."

27

Christopher was starting to feel that was true, but he also knew that they couldn't just ignore the obvious.

"We have to eliminate all the more mundane explanations for this," Christopher pointed out. "Especially when the obvious killer is currently behind bars."

"There's another explanation." Paige stopped in front of him, looking up into his eyes. "You and I both know what this is, and that we won't find answers looking here."

"What is it?" Christopher asked. He knew what Paige was driving at, but he wanted her to be the one to say the words. She was the expert on this, after all. He could see the gears turning in her head as she thought it through, obviously wanting to be certain before she just came out and said what she was thinking.

Finally, she seemed certain enough to go through with it.

"I think we have a copycat on our hands. The similarities in the MO are just too great. The same number of stab wounds, the same victim profile, the fact that victims were lured into position before the killer struck. One of those elements might be coincidence, and all of them might just be someone trying to cover up a normal murder if it were just the one killing, but two like this?"

Christopher could only nod along with Paige's reasoning, but the implications of it were terrifying. Someone just trying to cover up a murder by copying a serial killer would be bad enough, but a full-blown copycat might mean more deaths to follow, unless he and Paige found a way to stop the killer.

"If it is a copycat, what does that mean?" Christopher said. "Does it give us any way forward in all of this? Anything that might lead to the killer?"

"I think we need to know more about the original killings," Paige said. "I can remember a few details, but it isn't like I've had a chance to look at the files for those cases. Right now, I want to know *everything* about the murders Lars Ingram committed."

CHAPTER SIX

As far as Paige could see, almost nothing had changed about Christopher's office from the last time she'd been in there, when they'd been chasing Adam Riker. He still had the same corner office with a view out over D.C. that he'd had before. It still wasn't quite as large as it could have been, although that might have had something to do with the piles of clutter in it. Paperwork was still spread everywhere, in piles that gave Paige the urge to tidy up the moment that she looked at them.

There were glass boards up on one side of the room, one of them occupied by pictures of Zoe and Marta. A picture labelled Lars Ingram sat nearby, off to one side. He was a man in his forties, with square, almost bullish features, and a cold expression, pictured in an orange prison uniform.

Paige went to find a place to sit, moving one of the piles of paperwork off a chair.

"Hey, how am I meant to find anything if you move it around?" Christopher asked. Paige couldn't tell if he was being serious or not.

"Are you trying to tell me that you know where everything is?" Paige asked him. She'd known people like this at college, whose rooms had resembled the aftermath of an explosion in a stationery store every time they had a paper coming up. She hadn't believed that they knew where things were, either.

"I have a system," Christopher assured her. Paige would believe that when she saw it.

"Piles of stuff on the floor don't count as a system. Besides, I need somewhere to sit."

She took a chair and sat down, while Christopher planted himself behind the desk, in a space that seemed barely big enough to contain his height.

"Can you call up all the information on Lars Ingram's cases?" Paige asked.

"You asked about his cases before," Christopher said. "Why focus on him, though, when we know it can't be him? Doesn't it risk distracting from the actual killer?"

"If I'm right about this being a copycat, I want to see how much of it they got right, and if there are any differences." Those differences might allow them to identify their killer, focusing on what was unique about him, and hopefully identifying ways in which he hadn't been as careful as he should have been about protecting his identity. Copycats didn't always get the details right, only copying what they'd heard in the news.

"Ok," Christopher said, and started to tap in the details to call up Ingram's murders on his office computer.

Paige went around the desk to see the results, and she was only too aware of how close she was standing to him as she did so. Carefully, pointedly, Paige took a small step back, avoiding a stack of paperwork, just to remind herself that she had no business being so aware of anything when it came to Christopher.

Paige was still reminding herself of that when a man walked into the office. He was perhaps six feet tall, with salt and pepper hair and a short beard framing slender features. His frame was even more slender in a dark suit, a chrome plated watch flashing at his wrist as he moved.

"Marriott, there you are," he said. "What's this I hear about you drafting in someone from outside the BAU to help on your case?"

Paige saw Christopher stand. "Agent Sauer, this is Paige King, who helped me out with the Adam Riker manhunt. Paige, this is Agent Andrew Sauer, my immediate superior."

"*This* is who you've brought in?" Agent Sauer said, looking Paige up and down. "The same woman you had running around with you trying to catch up to Riker while he killed four more people? The one whose past ended up plastered all over the news channels?"

Paige didn't need the reminder that all the details of her past were out there, for anyone to find. The death of her father, the things that had happened with her stepfather, all of it.

"I believe that Riker would have gone on to kill more if it weren't for Paige's help," Christopher said.

It was obvious that his boss wasn't happy.

"Wait, didn't I hear that she was in training at the academy?"

"That's right," Paige said, determined to speak up for herself in this.

"So you've brought someone in on a case who's half trained? Who isn't qualified yet to do the job?"

Christopher was already shaking his head. "With respect, sir, Paige is *eminently* qualified when it comes to looking into the work of serial killers. She has a PhD in criminal psychology and has spent time working in an institution with some of the worst offenders out there. I believe that her insights will be invaluable."

"More valuable than those of the fully trained profilers we already have?" Sauer said, sounding as though he didn't quite believe it. Paige could understand that. She knew how well trained the profilers might be, because she'd seen for herself how hard even the basic training was.

"I believe so, sir."

Christopher's boss still didn't look convinced. "And what insights has she brought to the table so far?" He looked straight across at Paige, his gaze piercing. "I don't mean this as an insult, maybe you'll make it as an agent in time, once you're fully trained, but what have you done so far? What can you really tell me about this case?"

Paige knew that she had to say something quickly to convince this man if she wanted to be a part of the case. "That it was probably a copycat. That the murders appear consistent with those of Lars Ingram, who is currently on death row. That the victims have no obvious enemies, and that the killer struck in a very consistent way with both. More than that, he did it expertly, without leaving obvious trace evidence and while avoiding cameras at one scene. That suggests someone who has killed before, or at least committed other crimes."

Sauer looked as though he was relenting a little, but not completely. "And tell me about copycat killers."

It was obviously a test, clearly something that, as someone who worked within the BAU, he would already know about. Paige answered anyway, because she suspected that if she didn't impress this man, she was going to find herself sent back to the academy.

"The term 'copycat crime' was first coined in 1916, following a series of murders that appeared to imitate the earlier murders of Jack the Ripper," she said. "We know that several killers appear to have taken inspiration from TV series, while others have repeated the MOs of previous criminals, as with Eddie Seda copying the approach of the Zodiac Killer two decades after the first set of murders."

"So you can recite from a book," Sauer said. "Can you tell me what motivates these people, though?"

"Sir," Christopher said, obviously trying to defend her. "Paige is my choice for this. That should be-"

"What motivates them, Ms. King?" He obviously wasn't going to let it go.

31

Paige looked him in the eye, determined not to back down now. She was pretty sure that was a part of this man's test too, trying to see if she had the steel to do her part out in the field.

"It will vary from killer to killer," she said. "Assuming that all copycats, or all killers, are the same is a good way to miss the differences that might actually help to find them. But broadly, copycats can be motivated by a desire for fame, by admiration, or by the belief that copying a 'successful' model will make it more likely that they'll get away with their crimes."

"Go on," Sauer said.

"Fame is the most common motivator, with copycats focusing on the most publicly sensationalized cases," Paige said. "They hope that if they copy the methods of an infamous killer, it will make them just as notorious. There are also those who admire particular killers or become obsessed by them. For them, the repetition of someone else's method's is as much a part of their compulsion as the need to kill."

Sauer cocked his head to one side. "And the third category?"

"Those follow the example of previous crimes because they think it will let them stay free," Paige said. "Or because they have a desire to kill and copying someone else provides them with a roadmap of how to do it."

Now, Christopher *did* step in.

"Is that good enough for you, sir? Has she proven that she knows enough to be here?"

It was obvious that Christopher knew it was a test too.

What if Agent Sauer said no? Was it possible that Christopher's boss might just send her home, so soon after Paige had started work on this case? Would she have to return to the academy, try to catch up with whatever she'd missed, and just hope that she would get another shot when she finally completed her training? Paige found that she really didn't want to do that, not now that she was involved in this, not now that she'd seen the faces of the victims. She wanted to get justice for them.

Agent Sauer nodded. "Acceptable. All right, Marriott, it's your choice. If you really want this trainee to be your profiler on this, I'm not going to stop you. But that also means that *you're* the one who has to answer to the press for bringing her in if you don't succeed in catching this killer."

"Of course, sir," Christopher said. He didn't sound as if he had any doubts. Paige was glad one of them didn't.

Agent Sauer nodded curtly to Paige.

"Welcome to the team. I hope you're as good as Agent Marriott thinks you are."

He walked out of the office, not giving either of them a chance to say more.

Paige breathed a sigh of relief as he did so that she wasn't just being thrown off the team. She didn't know what to think of Agent Sauer. His initial hostility to her presence raised a note of dislike for him in her, but she could understand that it was just because he wanted the best people on the job.

That brought its own pressure, because it meant that Paige had to *be* the best person.

"Sorry about that," Christopher said. "I should have warned you that my superiors weren't exactly up to speed on all of this."

Paige would have appreciated a heads-up, certainly. "Are you *sure* that you want me on this?"

"That's one part of all of this that I'm certain of," Christopher said. "If anyone can help me find answers, it's you."

Paige hoped that she could live up to that kind of expectation, and not just because she didn't want to disappoint Christopher. They *had* to catch this killer.

As a start, she began to look through the files on Lars Ingram's murders, taking in the details of the cases one by one.

The most obvious link between all of the cases was clear from the start: all of the victims were young women who worked in the caring professions, all killed at night, all lured to a particular spot and stabbed the same number of times. That element seemed almost ritualistic, yet there was no sense of ritual to the rest of the crimes, only the precision of someone trying not to be caught by using a consistent method.

There didn't seem to be any *other* links that Paige could see. None of the victims knew one another according to the files. They didn't look alike, didn't have anything in common apart from their jobs and the way in which they'd been killed.

"It's a fairly tight geographical grouping around D.C.," Paige observed. Some of the killings spilled over into surrounding states, but not far. It seemed that Ingram had been able to find a steady supply of victims close at hand without having to look further afield.

"And now these two killings are here," Christopher said. "I wonder if that's because our copycat lives here, or if he's killing here as some kind of tribute to the original murders?"

"Probably the former," Paige guessed. "Copycats tend to kill in a place that's convenient for them, regardless of whether it has anything to do with the original killer. The guy who copied the Zodiac Killer did so in New York, when the original murders were around San Francisco. If he's killing in D.C., it's because he's *from* D.C."

Paige kept looking at the files, trying to see any differences between the old murders and the new. The truly worrying thing was that she couldn't. Everything about the murders, *everything,* matched. It was almost as if the same guy who had killed all of the first set of victims had simply continued his work.

That was impossible, though.

"This isn't right," Paige said. "It doesn't make sense."

"What isn't?"

"These murders are all too close to the originals. They don't get anything wrong."

Christopher frowned as she said that, obviously not understanding.

"I thought the *point* of a copycat was to be as close to the original as possible, particularly if they're going in for some kind of tribute act, rather than just trying for the fame," Christopher said.

"Yes, but this is murder, not music," Paige explained. "It's not like going onto the internet and learning a bunch of a band's songs note for note. The average copycat is working with what they can find out in the press, and that often gets misreported, or details are held back. This killer is copying Ingram exactly."

"So this guy is too perfect?" Christopher said.

Paige nodded. "Copycats get the general shape of a crime right, but they usually mess up the details. *This* killer has gotten the details right. They couldn't have gotten closer to it if Lars Ingram had talked them through the murders himself."

Paige found herself looking over at the photograph of Ingram up on the board, wondering if maybe, just maybe, there was some way that he had done exactly that.

"The only way that would be possible would be if the current killer had some kind of contact with Ingram," Christopher said, obviously understanding where Paige's thoughts were going.

"It's not the only way," Paige said. "It's possible that the reporting had enough details for someone to put this together, but… if there *has* been that contact, we might be able to trace it back to find the killer. At the very least, we need to know about the people around Ingram, to see if he ever had any acolytes or admirers."

The idea that a killer might have either was kind of sickening, but Paige knew that plenty of killers had both. There was something about the danger and transgression of what they did that attracted a certain kind of person.

"You know what that means we'll have to do?" Christopher asked. He sounded slightly worried, and Paige guessed that it was on her behalf.

Yes, she knew exactly what they needed to do next, and the thought of it made her swallow back a lump of fear in her throat. She was going to have to do something that she hadn't done since Adam Riker's escape. She was going to have to sit across a table from a serial killer and try to understand him.

"I know," Paige said. "We're going to have to go speak to Lars Ingram."

CHAPTER SEVEN

Paige had spent plenty of time working inside a secure mental institution, but that was still a far cry from the penitentiary that she and Christopher made their way through, going to see Lars Ingram.

This didn't pretend to be calming and serene with pastel colors the way the institute had. Instead, the surfaces were institutional gray and harsh white, the bars solid and the guards watching warily as Paige and Christopher made their way into a waiting area that was pretty much empty at the moment. Apparently, they weren't here for usual visiting hours.

The receptionist was a woman in her fifties, wearing a floral print dress and dark cardigan that seemed slightly at odds with the surroundings.

"Yes?" she said. "What can I do for you?"

Paige saw Christopher take out his ID to show to the receptionist.

"Agent Marriott with the FBI. I called ahead. My associate and I are here to see Lars Ingram."

"I'll just check the system," the receptionist said, and typed something quickly into a computer in front of her. "Ah, yes. It's all here. Looks like you're just in time."

"What does that mean?" Paige asked, not quite understanding.

The receptionist looked at her strangely, as if surprised that she didn't know already. "Lars Ingram's execution is scheduled for tomorrow night."

Paige had known that he was due to die soon in general terms, but the closeness of the date took her a little by surprise. It meant that the pressure on this meeting was suddenly increased a hundred times over. They would probably only have one chance to get anything out of Ingram, and if they blew it, there would never be another opportunity, because he would be dead.

"If you'll take a seat, a guard will be here to escort you soon."

Paige sat down with Christopher just a seat away, far too aware of how close he was. To distract herself, she asked about Ingram.

"Do you think he'll actually be able to give us the other killer?" Paige asked. She was hoping for a lead, but would Ingram be able to go further and just give them a name?

"I hope so. Like you said, this new killer seems to know too much about his methods. That suggests that maybe they've had some contact. The only question is how we get that information out of him."

Christopher didn't sound entirely hopeful when it came to that.

"You think it will be a problem?" Paige said.

She saw the FBI agent shrug. "Ingram doesn't have anything to gain here. He's on death row, he knows that there's nothing we can do for him. Nothing that will make his life easier, no chance of commuting his sentence. We can't even pretend that we can, when his death is already scheduled. We'll need to think of something else if we're going to get him to talk."

Paige tried to imagine what that might be. What did a serial killer like Ingram want? The truth was that the answer to a question like that was always complex and would probably have taken her several sessions as a psychologist to even begin to figure out. Now, she had to guess it in just one, and successfully find a way to leverage it. Did he want fame? Control? Was there some kind of deep reason behind all of it relating to his past? Paige didn't know.

"Do you think it's significant that the killings have taken place so close to Ingram's execution?" Paige asked. The timing of it all seemed far too specific to be a coincidence.

Christopher nodded. "It's hard to see how they couldn't be linked. Maybe the copycat heard about Ingram because he's scheduled for execution, and that's what prompted him to start killing?"

It was possible. Copycats sometimes came out of the most sensational coverage, so maybe the coverage of Ingram leading up to his execution had sparked something in the wrong person. Yet it was also possible that this was an existing copycat who was escalating around the date of the execution as some kind of tribute to the serial killer, or that it was a coincidence, brought about by some outside influence that Paige and Christopher didn't know about.

That was the problem with all of this: there was no way to narrow down the possibilities. Right then, the important point was to find the copycat, and that meant trying to get answers out of Lars Ingram as quickly as possible.

A guard came to collect them, a woman in her twenties, solidly built with her blonde hair hacked short. She offered them a smile.

"Are you two the FBI agents here to see Lars Ingram?"

Paige was about to point out that she wasn't an FBI agent yet, but Christopher got there first.

"Yes, that's us. I'm Agent Marriott, and this is Paige King."

Paige felt strangely grateful that Christopher didn't spend time spelling out that she was just a trainee, that she didn't really deserve to be there. He didn't make her feel like she was an outsider.

"I'm Nadia. Follow me."

The guard led the way out of the waiting area, through a security checkpoint and then deeper into the prison.

"You'll be meeting Ingram in the room on death row we reserve for meetings with lawyers and family," the guard said. "With such dangerous prisoners, we don't bring them to the usual visiting rooms."

It seemed like a sensible precaution to Paige, but it also meant that she and Christopher had to go far deeper into the prison, walking along halls lined with cells. Paige could feel the eyes of the prisoners on her as she went.

"Hey, pretty girl! You here for some fun?"

It reminded her far too much of her time in the institution, with that familiar feeling of very dangerous people looking at her like she was a potential target. It was a frightening sensation, especially now that Paige had seen exactly how dangerous the attentions of someone like that could be thanks to Adam Riker. He'd fixated on her, escaped from the institution that held him, then targeted people from Paige's life he thought had wronged her, all building up to the moment when he tried to force her to kill her own mother.

At the same time, though, Paige knew that she had to be tougher about this. Christopher didn't seem to have a problem walking through this place, and nor did the guard leading them.

Paige kept her eyes forward and kept walking, trying to make herself look as little like prey to these violent men as possible.

They headed deeper into the prison, past the general wings, into a space that was smaller and quieter, but which instantly felt more oppressive. Paige knew instantly that they were on death row now. She would have known it just from the looks of the orange-jumpsuitwearing prisoners there. They were a whole order of danger greater than those of the prisoners in the rest of the prison. They were the expressions of men who had nothing left to lose, and so no reason to hold back from any violence that they wanted.

"Don't go near the bars," the guard with them said.

"They like to attack if you get too close?" Christopher asked.

Paige saw her nod, and wondered what it had to be like, working every day in a place where she might be attacked or even killed. Then again, Paige was planning to join the FBI, and she had no illusions about that keeping her safe.

"We search the cells regularly, and we find improvised weapons far too often," Nadia said.

The guard led them through to an interview room in the same drab gray as the rest of the place. There was a camera on one wall, and a table in the middle with a screen set halfway down it. There were chairs on either side, while metal brackets on the table were obviously designed to allow a prisoner to be handcuffed in place.

"Wait here," the guard said. "Don't leave this room without me. It won't be safe."

Paige sat, waiting with Christopher on the far side of the screen. It meant that she got a good view of the door as Lars Ingram came in, led by the guard.

He was a little over six feet tall, with a face that was lined and worn from his time in custody. His hair was cropped short, revealing scars on one side of his face. His large frame seemed almost slumped in on itself as he walked, but Paige wasn't fooled by that. She could see the anger lurking in his expression as he looked over at her and Christopher. She suspected that the slumped look was a way to lure people in closer, getting where he wanted to be in order to do damage.

The guard sat him down and cuffed his hands to the table. He looked over at Paige and Christopher but didn't say anything.

"Lars Ingram, I'm Agent Marriott, and this is Ms. King," Christopher said, in a formal, professional tone. "We'd like to ask you some questions."

He gave a kind of grunt before he answered, as if the whole thing were an effort for him. "About what?"

"There have been two murders in the last few days," Christopher said.

"And why should I care?" Ingram demanded.

"Because those murders have stolen your MO," Paige said. "Someone is copying you, Lars."

She used his first name deliberately, trying to establish a connection, however small.

He shrugged then. "If you're here looking for suspects, I have a pretty good alibi."

It was obviously a joke, but there was nothing funny about him in that moment. He was looking at Paige with contempt, but also with something far more dangerous. Paige knew that look: it was the expression of someone looking her over like he was determining what kind of a target she would make.

"We're not here for you, Lars," Paige said. "We want to find who's copying you."

This time, the look was almost pure disdain.

"And why should I care about that? You going to offer me a pardon if I help you? A stay of execution? You *know* what I'm facing tomorrow, right?"

Christopher shook his head. "We don't have the authority to offer you anything."

"Then why should I talk to you?" Ingram demanded. "Why shouldn't I just go back to my cell and think about what I'm having for my last meal?"

Paige caught the moment when Christopher looked over at her. He was obviously hoping that she would be able to find a way to get Ingram to talk. That was the reason that she was here, after all: to get inside the heads of serial killers. If she couldn't do that, here, then was she really going to be able to help find the man who'd done this?

Paige took her best shot, trying to work out what drove this man, and what he would react to.

"Are you happy that someone is copying you, Lars?" Paige asked, trying to play on his pride. "You killed in a way that was special to you, that meant something to you, yet here is someone else stealing that from you, sullying your work with their own."

It was a shot in the dark, but Paige thought that perhaps it might work. Some killers were proud of their work to the extent that they might consider anyone who tried to copy it a threat to their legacy. They wanted to be unique.

The shot didn't land, though. Paige could see that it didn't, because Ingram just shrugged.

"It doesn't matter to me if someone else copies me. It's kind of flattering," Ingram said. "Maybe I should be *happy* that someone wants to do things my way. Stop wasting my time."

Paige swallowed, trying to think of another approach to try. She looked over at Christopher in case he wanted to take over, but he just gave her an encouraging look. Paige went again.

"You've talked about how little time you have left a couple of times now," she said. "Just one more day. And what have you actually achieved in your life? All you've done is evil. This is your last chance to do something good. Something worthwhile."

For a second or two, Ingram was silent. The silence just deepened, and Paige thought that maybe, just maybe she'd managed to get through to him.

Then Ingram laughed.

"Is *that* all you've got? You think I feel guilty? Every single one of those bitches was asking for it. The only regret I have is that I didn't get more of them. Guard! Take me back to my cell!"

"Wait, we're not done here," Paige said.

"Yes, we are," Ingram said. The guard came forward, unlocking him from the table. He stood. "You know what? A guy wants to keep killing, good for him."

He headed for the door, and the only thing Paige felt then was a yawning chasm of emptiness. Christopher had been relying on her to find a way to get through to Ingram, but she'd just run straight into a brick wall. She'd failed. All she could do was watch as the guard took Ingram away, ready to return him to his cell.

She wanted to be able to call out after him in that moment, to come up with something clever that would get him to talk, but the truth was that she couldn't think of anything. Paige and Christopher had struck out here. They weren't going to get any help with the copycat from the man he was copying.

All they could do now was try to come up with something else, but Paige couldn't even begin to think of what.

CHAPTER EIGHT

It felt strange, to be stalking another victim so soon after his last. Before, he'd left it months between each one, if not longer. He'd make a kill, and then there would be a gap in which he could enjoy the sensations of peace and fulfilment that came from doing it. There was always a kind of joy that came from a kill, and normally he took his time in basking in it.

Now, though, with Lars Ingram's execution looming, he didn't have the time to waste like that. He had to act. He had a lot of work to do if he was going to accomplish everything he had to in time.

Yet there were some things that couldn't be rushed.

Currently, he was sitting outside a café, watching a young woman wrangle two small children with a kind of expertise that would almost have been impressive if he had cared about such things.

He didn't care, except about the fact that *she* cared. She sold that caring, as an au pair to the von Ryan family. It made her a target.

Amelie Pichou, twenty. Pretty, he had to admit that, with delicate features and a button nose. Not that it mattered much. It wasn't about the looks of the people he killed. This wasn't a date.

No, it was much more intimate than that. The most intimate moment that Amelie would ever have in her life.

As Amelie led the children down the street, he followed her, staying back, watching her. This part was about learning everything he could about her. About observing her, the way she reacted, the things that might be useful when he made his move. He wanted to know what would lure her into place, what would give him the time he needed to make those precise seven strikes with the knife, exactly the way that Lars Ingram had made them.

He had the knife on him now. It would have been easy to walk up and kill her, there in the street. He could have done it and walked off before anyone even reacted.

Two things stopped him. The first was that he was always more cautious than that. He had no intention of getting caught. Here, in the street, there would be witnesses and cameras. He'd become expert at avoiding both. One of the reasons that he'd taken to copying Lars Ingram's work was that he'd been so successful.

Ingram had managed to strike again and again like a ghost because he'd picked those who were likely to be isolated, surrounded only by people they were there to care for, not those who could try to protect them. Ingram had managed to get into homes without being seen, and without leaving so much as a trace of evidence behind him until that last fateful day.

He was determined to be more careful than that. *He* wouldn't leave DNA behind.

The second reason was that he wanted to do Lars Ingram's methods justice. He wanted to honor the man who was his inspiration, and *that* meant doing things exactly the way he would have done them. It meant breaking in exactly the way he would, luring his victims to the perfect place, finishing them with the same knife wounds to the same places.

There was a kind of deep satisfaction that came from getting those details perfect. It wasn't a ritual, exactly. It felt like playing a difficult piece of music perfectly, getting every note correct.

Doing that meant he needed information, which was why he kept following Amelie, keeping far enough back that she wouldn't notice, and crucially, that anyone watching cameras later wouldn't be able to spot him tailing her. Not that anyone looked. People never looked properly. Amelie certainly didn't look around to see him following her.

She went back to the von Ryans' house, and he followed as far as he could. It was a large but modern structure, with elegant lines and long banks of windows looking out onto the rest of the city, and over small but well-tended gardens.

He found a spot not far from the house where he could watch it, sitting on a bench and pretending to look at his phone while he secretly used it to take photographs, trying to get a sense of the layout of the place. He took his time, noting the locations of the cameras around the perimeter of the house, then trying to work out exactly what fell in their fields of vision.

It would be a more difficult entry than it had been with the Estrom place. Certainly more difficult than the retirement home. Clearly the von Ryans took their security more seriously. Yet, he suspected that it would be possible to disable one of the cameras without being seen, and from there, he should have a route to get inside.

Of course, if the house had been full of people, it still wouldn't have worked. Even as he watched, he saw Amelie bring the children up to their mother and father, saw the children run around them boisterously. If all five of them were in the house, then it would create far too many opportunities for him to be seen. There would be too many uncontrolled elements.

That was why, when he'd been picking his target, one of the first things he'd done was to call up Amelie Pichou's social media accounts, and those of her employers. On her account, he hadn't found much that would be useful, but on Ms. von Ryan's accounts, he'd found everything he needed: all the details of the ski trip to San Moritz they were taking with the children. At *that* point, the fact that Amelie had plans in the city tomorrow had become very relevant: the au pair wasn't going with them.

Tonight, she would be in the house alone, probably enjoying everything that went with a place like this. Probably pretending that she owned the house for one night.

He watched her guide the children inside, continuing to take pictures as she led them through the house. It meant that he could get a sense of the routes she took through the place, and the room she went back to once the children were safely playing. He scanned the house, looking for the perfect spot in which to make his kill.

It was perhaps another ten minutes before he was satisfied that he had everything he needed. He knew that he had to leave then, though. It was probably wise not to sit here too long. People tended to notice more in affluent neighborhoods. Standing, he started to walk away.

He would be back though. Tonight, he would return, and then Amelie Pichou would die.

CHAPTER NINE

They had to wait while the guard took Lars back to his cell, which meant Paige continued sitting there in the interview room in the prison, trying to work out what she and Christopher were going to do next. She felt completely frustrated in that moment. She should have been able to get more out of Ingram.

"If we can't get this guy's identity out of Ingram, we're going to have to look for other ways to find it," Christopher said.

"I should have been able to get him to talk," Paige said. She felt as if she should be apologizing to Christopher for everything she'd just failed to do. "I read him wrong."

Christopher shook his head. "You gave it your best shot. I heard what you tried. They were both good shots. They just didn't land. You heard what he said at the end. He has nothing left to lose. He just doesn't care."

"*I* care," Paige said.

"And that's good," Christopher said. "But what we really need now is to find another way to get to the answers we need, and I don't know if we're going to find them here."

Paige shared his frustration, because they had to just sit here rather than getting on with hunting down the next lead. Except that Paige wasn't sure what that lead was going to be.

"We looked over the crime scenes, we have the coroner's report, what's next?" Paige asked.

"We don't have any physical leads so far," Christopher said. "So you tell me. You might not have gotten anything out of Ingram, but I'm pretty sure that you're the person best placed to get into the copycat's head."

After the way she'd struck out with Ingram, Paige wasn't so sure, but she gave it her best shot anyway.

"He's a copycat, but he's not *just* a copycat. He's precise about it. He knows all the details of the crimes. That says one of two things..." Paige had to think for a moment as the implications of it settled in her head "...either he was getting details straight from Ingram, or he was *completely* obsessed. Maybe a little of both. Someone that obsessed would want to get in contact, would want to let his hero know what he was doing, right?"

"That sounds plausible," Christopher said. "Which means we're in exactly the right place."

Paige frowned slightly before she understood what Christopher meant by that.

"Every phone call here is monitored," Christopher explained. "All the letters are opened and copied. There are visitor logs, call records. The prisoners don't have the same rights to privacy that everyone else does, so we can potentially go through it all. If we're lucky, then our guy will be in there."

Paige felt a lot more hopeful than she had just a few minutes ago. Before, they'd had nothing, but now, they had something to go on, somewhere to look. She had to believe that a copycat would want to get in touch with Ingram. There was a level of infatuation to someone like that which wouldn't allow them to hold back. Even if they didn't need to get more details from Ingram, having gotten them some other way, they would have to find some way to at least express their admiration.

The guard, Nadia, came back after a few minutes. "Ok, if you're ready to go, then I'll lead you back out."

"Actually," Christopher said, "We need to go through any communications Lars Ingram has received. I want to look at the phone records, the letters, all of it."

"I can take you to the admin offices. Everything should be there."

She led the way back out through the prison. Paige felt the eyes on her there again, watching her every move. It made her grateful that she didn't have to work in a place like this anymore. She vastly preferred being out in the world, trying to actually catch killers, rather than being in the places they were locked up.

The guard led the way up through the prison, into a set of run-down offices that looked as if they hadn't been renovated in years. Those offices were filled with staff. There were several guards there, but more clerks. She led the way to one of them.

"Krista, these people are with the FBI. They're asking for access to an inmate's correspondence. Can I leave them to you? I have to get back to work."

Paige saw the clerk nod.

"I'll have to check with the warden, but it should be fine. Which prisoner?"

"Lars Ingram," Christopher said. "We're looking to work out who might have been in contact with him."

"I'll check with the warden, then find the letters for you and call up the visitor records."

It felt pretty strange to Paige, the ease with which they were able to get so much information about a prisoner. She'd spent plenty of time at the FBI academy going through all the legal limits on their powers as agents, all the protections that were there specifically to prevent any kind of abuse of power.

She had to remind herself that those protections didn't apply to prisoners in the same way, that they'd been specifically excluded to ensure that prisoners couldn't continue to order crimes from inside.

It meant that when the clerk came back, it was with a thick file, filled with letters, seeming almost to overflow with them. Paige had to admit, she was surprised by just how much correspondence Lars Ingram seemed to have.

"This should be everything," Krista said, setting it down on one of the desks. "I'll pull up the rest of the information on my terminal for you to look at."

She sat down and typed something in. "There, it should be all set for you."

Christopher went to the computer, obviously wanting to take that side of things. "I'll go through the visitor records and call logs, then check the names to see if there's anyone who visited him who doesn't fit. Can you go through the letters? I think you're the best person to try to identify anyone who's obsessed enough to potentially be our copycat."

Paige nodded. "I can do that."

Obsession shouldn't be too hard to spot, at least not when it came to the kind that might push someone into being a copycat killer.

She started to go through the letters. The first few were legal letters, sent from his attorney, appearing to discuss his attempts to appeal or seek clemency. Paige saw the words "we regret to inform you that your appeal has been denied due to a lack of new evidence" repeated again and again. It seemed that Lars Ingram, or at least his lawyers, had scrambled to try to keep him alive. There were other letters from the ACLU, and from groups protesting more because they opposed the death penalty in principle than because they actually cared about Lars Ingram specifically.

Paige still had to read through them, in case there were any signs of an obsessive fan hidden somewhere within the letters, in case there was anything in the letters from the lawyers that shouldn't have been there. If there was anything too personal, anything that didn't fit the work of a lawyer, Paige was determined to pick it out.

There wasn't anything in the lawyers' letters, though, just the progress of the legal system towards the inevitability of Lars Ingram's execution, in spite of their efforts to prevent it.

Paige moved on to the other letters. There weren't any from Ingram's family. If he still had any left, then they clearly didn't want anything to do with him, or with the horrific acts he'd committed. Apparently, even the people who loved him most had accepted the monster he was.

There were letters from people who wanted to say exactly that to Ingram, their letters spelling out all the ways that they thought even execution wasn't good enough for him. He'd gotten what seemed like plenty of hate mail.

Yet there were also letters there that seemed to go the other way. There were letters from a woman somewhere in Texas expressing her love and admiration for him.

You're the first thing that I think about in the morning. You don't deserve to be in prison. I know I could change you, and that we could be happy together. If I were there, I'd…

"Look up a woman named Elaine Williamson," Paige said to Christopher. "She's sent Ingram letters expressing her deep love and admiration. Some of them are… well, pretty explicit."

"Do you think she's a possibility?" Christopher asked as he started to input her name.

"I'm not sure," Paige said. "I *think* she's probably just one of those people who fall in love with inmates."

That happened. Paige had read about plenty of cases, and even seen a couple when she was working back at the institute. People saw killers and criminals on the news, and there was something about that exposure that attracted people who were missing something in their lives. People who projected those needs onto others and assumed that the worst kind of killers had everything that they needed.

"But is it possible that she's gone further?"

That was the key question.

"Maybe," Paige said. "Generally, these people are more likely to turn out to be additional victims of criminals if they ever get out, but I

48

guess it's just about possible that this woman might be obsessed enough to want to copy Ingram's crimes. The one thing I *don't* like is that she's from Texas."

"And you told me before that copycats don't usually change their location before they start killing," Christopher said. Paige was pleased by the fact that he'd listened to what she'd said about copycats.

"There's no sign of her on the visitor lists, or on the call logs," Christopher said. "Give me a second. I'm going to try checking her social media accounts."

Paige waited expectantly, but it was less than a minute before Christopher shook his head.

"Her most recent social media posts have location markers. She's still in Texas."

Meaning that there was no way she could have been the one to kill two victims in Washington over the last couple of days. She had an alibi. Paige needed to keep looking.

There were other letters, expressing sympathy, or expressing hatred. None of them seemed like enough to indicate the kind of obsession that Paige and Christopher were looking for, the kind of obsession that might propel someone to kill, and to copy the methods that Ingram had used.

Paige continued to sift through the letters. There were more than she had thought that there might be. She had assumed that a killer locked away on death row wouldn't get much mail, but the pile was a thick one, taking in correspondence relating to Ingram's affairs, the progress of his appeals, and what Paige could only describe as fan mail.

It was that collection of letters that Paige delved more deeply into, reading through them one by one, trying to find anything that seemed as if it might be obsessive enough to indicate the work of a fellow killer.

Trying to diagnose that from just letters was a much harder task than Paige could have imagined, though. She was starting to think that it might be impossible.

Then Paige saw a letter that made her pause, reading through it again and again.

I wanted to write to you because I think what you did is amazing. I know people don't understand. They don't get that it takes real power to do what you did. That a strong man must make his own morality and do as he pleases.

Those bitches deserved what they got. I wish I could have been there with you when you did it, could have experienced everything you did as they died. What I wouldn't give for just one drink in O'Kelly's with you, so you could tell me all about it.

It was pretty intense, but there was another one just below it that was worse.

I want to know everything about how you did it. I understand everything you felt, I feel as if I have so many of the same feelings. I keep going to O'Kelly's, sitting in your seat, thinking about each of your kills moment by moment. If I'd been there, I want to think that I would have killed them exactly the same way. I feel a kind of connection to you, something special. You might be in prison now, but your work will go on.

"I think I've found someone," Paige said, feeling quite confident this time. "Isaac Coleridge. Judging by the address on the letters, he's from D.C."

More than close enough to be the one doing this.

"I'm checking him now," Christopher said. He typed for a few seconds. "His name is on the visitor records. He came to the prison to speak to Lars Ingram. Not just once, but a couple of times."

That fact made excitement start to build inside Paige. They had a man who had come to speak to Ingram, who had praised his work, who had expressed a wish that he could be there beside Ingram while he killed. A man who had been to the prison to speak to him multiple times, which suggested that it wasn't just a case of him showing up and being sent away by Ingram. They'd had something to talk about, and Paige could imagine exactly what that was.

"You think this our guy?" Paige asked Christopher, wanting the confirmation that she wasn't imagining how bad this looked for Isaac Coleridge.

"I was about to ask you that," he replied.

"I think he's definitely a suspect," Paige said. "At the very least, we need to speak to him."

"I agree," Christopher said. "We'll head over to Isaac Coleridge and find out *exactly* what his role in all of this is."

CHAPTER TEN

Paige could feel her sense of tension building as they drove to Isaac Coleridge's home address to question him. If they were lucky, they would be able to catch him out in a lie, or spot evidence somewhere in his home that would tie him to the scenes.

They stopped outside the dingy apartment building that Isaac Coleridge lived in. Paige looked it over, taking in the broken window on the ground floor, the overflowing trashcan out front. There was a homeless looking guy sitting near the steps leading up to the door.

Paige and Christopher approached the building slowly, watching for trouble. Christopher hit the button on the intercom for Isaac Coleridge's place. There was no answer. In a place like this, it might just mean that the intercom was broken. It could also mean that Isaac Coleridge had seen them coming and was keeping his head down.

Christopher seemed to be thinking the same thing. He turned to the homeless guy, reaching into his pocket. Paige thought that he might come out with his ID, but he got his wallet out instead, taking out a twenty.

"This is your regular spot, right?"

"I guess."

"So you know the people who live here?"

That got a shrug from the homeless guy.

Christopher held out the bill, and also held up a photograph, taken from the DMV. It showed a flabby featured man with dark, lank hair and with something about him that just seemed... wrong, to Paige.

"Isaac Coleridge."

The homeless guy took it and made a face. "I know him. What about him?"

"Is he here? Have you seen him leave?" Christopher asked.

The homeless guy shrugged again. "Left earlier this morning. Gone to work, I guess. Weird guy."

"How is he weird?" Paige asked.

The homeless guy cocked his head to one side. "Just... weird."

It wasn't exactly a helpful description, but then, how much would this man really see of Isaac? At the same time though, he'd probably had to develop pretty good instincts about people while he was living on the streets, just to keep away from the ones who were dangerous.

"We need to find out where he works," Paige said to Christopher, as the two of them started to make their way back to the car.

"I'm already on it," Christopher said, typing something into his phone. "Got it. Apparently, he works at a local marketing firm."

They drove over there, and Paige took the time to research Coleridge while Christopher picked their way through traffic. There were no arrest records for him that Paige could find, no sign that he'd been involved in anything shady. The public parts of his social media showed a love of extreme metal, artisanal beer, and horror movies, along with a knack for saying whatever seemed most controversial at the time, apparently just so that he could wade into the ensuing comment war.

The firm he worked at was in a nicer part of D.C. than his apartment, but only a little. This was apparently not a guy whose talents had taken him to one of the major D.C. companies. Instead, the firm he worked for was tucked away in an aging building on a side street, which looked as if they'd tried to update it without much success.

Paige and Christopher headed inside, walking up to a reception desk staffed by a young woman in her twenties, wearing a purple cashmere sweater and jeans. Apparently, this was a dress down kind of office. Christopher held out his ID.

"Agent Marriott, FBI. I'm looking for Isaac Coleridge. Is he in the building?"

The receptionist blinked at the sight of the ID for a second or two, then seemed to get over her surprise at having the FBI there.

"Him?" she said, with a note of disgust. "No, he's not 'in the building.'"

Something about the way she said that caught Paige's attention. "Why? What happened?"

"He was let go," the receptionist said. "About a week ago."

Paige wanted more than that. "Why?"

The receptionist looked around as if she wasn't sure that she should really say anything, but then looked back towards Christopher's badge, as if trying to work out just how serious all of this was. Finally, she nodded, obviously making a decision.

"He was fired because of how weird he was being to the women who work here," the receptionist said. "He'd hit on them, send them these creepy messages, try to bully them. He sent *me* a picture of my

52

own front door. Like he was trying to say 'I know where you live' or something."

Paige froze, looking across to Christopher. It was hard to miss the significance of something like that. A man who admired the likes of Lars Ingram might find that being fired recently was exactly the spark he needed to push him over into murder. The more she heard about Isaac Coleridge, the more he sounded like exactly the kind of guy who might be committing these copycat murders.

The only problem now was finding him. The two of them walked out onto the sidewalk, the problem obvious.

"So Coleridge isn't at home, and he isn't at work," Paige said.

"We need to work out where he is," Christopher said, as they headed back out to the car. "If he is our guy, he might be stalking another victim already."

That was a worrying thought. Paige had assumed that the murders now had something to do with Lars Ingram's upcoming execution, but what if it was just one man embarking on a spree after being fired? He would try to kill quickly, targeting victims one after another, until he was caught.

They *had* to find him. The only question was where. Where would a man like Isaac Coleridge go when he had nowhere *to* go? When his work had fired him, but he wasn't at home, where did he have left to go?

One possibility was that he was out stalking another victim. That wasn't a helpful thought, though, because it meant that he could be anywhere in the city. Instead, Paige found her mind drawn to another possibility. Where would a man completely obsessed with Lars Ingram go? Where was the one place he'd mentioned *wanting* to go, in his letters?

"Coleridge mentioned a bar called O'Kelly's in his correspondence with Ingram," Paige said. "One Ingram supposedly frequented. It's possible that he might have gone there to feel closer to his 'hero.'"

Christopher seemed to weigh it up. "It's not a lot to go on, but it's the best we have right now. If he isn't there, then we'll have to get the techs to ping his cell phone or try to find him with facial recognition on cameras."

Both options that suggested he was taking the possibility of Ingram being a suspect very seriously indeed.

*

53

O'Kelly's bar turned out to be the owner's idea of a traditional Irish pub, complete with dirty painted glass in the windows and chalkboard outside proclaiming its selection of craft beers. Inside, it was dim and grimy, with a dartboard in the corner and a bar running most of the length of the far wall. Even at this hour of the day, there was a selection of patrons sitting around the place, some with beers in front of them, but more just hanging out, drinking coffee and eating bacon sandwiches.

Everything about the bar said to Paige that it was a dive, right down to the way the patrons' eyes tracked her and Christopher as they made their way to the bar, not unfriendly, exactly, but definitely suspicious.

Paige looked around, trying to locate Isaac. He wasn't at the bar and didn't appear to be in any of the booths. For a moment or two, she thought that they'd come to the wrong place, but she still wanted to check.

Christopher clearly did too. He stepped up to the bar, setting his ID down on it.

"What can I do for you, Agent?" the bartender asked. He was an older man with thinning hair, wearing a grubby shirt and cleaning a glass with a cloth. He said it loud enough for the various patrons of the bar to hear, as if warning them not to say anything too incriminating.

"We're looking for someone," Christopher said. "Isaac Coleridge. We're told that he drinks here."

That was obviously a stretch. They didn't know for sure that Coleridge actually spent time there, but it seemed likely, and Paige knew that sometimes, it was better to sound as if you already knew the answers before you started asking questions.

"Don't know the name," the bartender said, but there was something about the flat way he said it that made Paige think that he might have said that if Christopher had asked him about his own mother. This wasn't the kind of bar where people cooperated with the police.

It was kind of irrelevant at that point, though, because that was when Paige saw Isaac Coleridge step back into the bar from the restrooms at the back. He was a bulky man in a leather jacket and stained t-shirt with the logo of a band Paige didn't know. He was probably a little under six feet tall and wore a heavy collection of rings on each hand.

"There!" Paige said, touching Christopher on the shoulder and pointing.

Coleridge took one look at them there and ran, heading straight back towards the restrooms.

Paige realized her mistake in an instant. She'd needed to tell Christopher that she'd spotted him, but the way she'd done it had only given him a chance to flee. It meant that she and Christopher had to barrel through the bar, dodging around tables and heading for the back.

They got there in time for Paige to see Coleridge running out of a back door into an alley. She followed, with Christopher a pace or two in front of her, bursting out into a dirty alley behind the bar. Coleridge was already heading for another, moving faster than his overweight frame suggested he should be able to.

One of the tests to get into the FBI Academy had been a timed 300-yard sprint, the distance apparently based on the length a chase might normally go before a suspect ran out of options. Paige had gotten through it but had been a long way from the fastest in her class, and now she found Christopher pulling away from her as he kept up the pursuit down the length of the second alley, dodging around dumpsters as Coleridge kept going.

Paige did her best to keep up. She might not be the best at the physical aspects of the training, but if Christopher was going to tackle this guy, she wanted him to have some kind of backup.

The three of them turned a corner, with Coleridge in front and the two of them following on behind. Paige could see him starting to slow now, obviously not used to this kind of exertion. She was still able to keep going; she hadn't realized just how much the training had improved her base level of fitness in the time she'd been at the academy.

Coleridge slowed now, and Christopher was almost level with him, lunging forward to tackle him to the ground. Paige was there in a couple of strides, helping to grab one of his arms, wrenching it behind his back so that Christopher could cuff him.

Before, Paige had been suspicious, and now that Coleridge had run, that suspicion had only increased.

"Isaac Coleridge?" Christopher said. "We have some questions we need to ask you about the murders of Marta Huarez and Zoe Wells."

CHAPTER ELEVEN

Paige found herself eager to get answers out of Isaac Coleridge as they took him back to the FBI to question him, putting him in a clean, modern interrogation room and leaving him there watched by cameras while they tried to work out the best strategy to get him to talk.

"We'll leave him to sweat a little longer," Christopher said, with a nod towards the screen that held the feeds from the cameras. "You can see that he's nervous, so maybe that will encourage him to talk."

He *did* look nervous to Paige, face flushed, obviously sweating with the stress of being in there. He hadn't asked for a lawyer yet, but Paige had no doubt that he would, soon enough.

She found it interesting, though, that he *was* so nervous. Serial killers were usually better at hiding their emotions than that, if they even felt them the same way. Some of the more recent research suggested that for psychopaths, there was typically less development in the amygdala than for most people, resulting not just in a lack of empathy, but also in lower feelings of fear or anxiety.

Sitting there scared in an interview room didn't fit with that. Of course, it was possible that Isaac wasn't a psychopath. It wasn't strictly necessary to be a serial killer, although most were. It was possible that his obsession with Lars Ingram was simply great enough to push him over the barrier to killing someone.

Even so, Paige found the fact that he was so nervous… odd. There was definitely more to be asked there.

"I want to learn everything possible about his life before we go in there," Christopher said.

That was another standard tactic, and one that Paige had learned about at the academy. The more it was possible to show a suspect that you already had information, the less likely they were to lie, because they tended to assume that you already knew the truth.

Paige was willing to go along with it, getting out her computer and researching what she could on Isaac Coleridge. There wasn't much that she and Christopher hadn't already looked up. No criminal record. Graduated from a community college. His social media didn't show many signs of past girlfriends but *did* show that he'd gone from job to job at a pace that suggested he didn't really fit in anywhere.

"How long do you want to leave him?" Paige asked. She trusted Christopher's judgement in this, but she was eager to get in there and talk to Isaac. If they were lucky, he was their guy, and they would be able to get a confession out of him before the end of the day. The victims would have the justice they deserved, and a killer would be off the streets for good.

"I think he's waited long enough," Christopher said. He led the way into the interrogation room, and Paige followed close behind. Neither of them said anything for now. Instead, they both sat down in silence opposite Isaac, letting the tension there build.

"Why did you run when you saw us, Isaac?" Christopher asked at last. He was obviously trying to drive home just how guilty that made Isaac seem, cutting through any hope he had of just denying everything.

"Wouldn't *you* run if you saw the cops?" Isaac shot back.

"FBI, Isaac, not cops," Christopher corrected him. Again, Paige had the feeling that it was designed to ramp up the pressure on him.

Looking at him, though, Paige wasn't sure that he needed more pressure. She could see the way his hands were shaking, and the way he was sweating. This was someone who was obviously terrified.

She might have had more sympathy for him if she didn't suspect that he'd murdered two women.

She could see Christopher looking over at her, obviously looking for a way that would let them open up Isaac Coleridge, getting him to talk. She suspected that challenging him with the crimes wouldn't work, not yet. He would only deny them. She had to think of a more oblique way to approach it.

"Tell us about Lars Ingram," she said.

He looked at her, obviously nonplussed. "What?"

"You're his biggest fan, aren't you? You sent him letters to tell him that. You even went to visit him in prison."

He stared at her then, eyes widening. "How... how do you know that?"

"We checked the prison records," Christopher said. "After someone killed two women using Lars Ingram's MO."

It was more direct than Paige would have preferred, but she could see the point of the question, obviously seeking to let Isaac know just how much trouble he was in, not giving him any room in which to squirm out.

57

"What?" Isaac said, looking around in something close to panic. "You think that I…"

"We think that you killed them," Paige said. "You're obviously obsessed with Ingram. We think obsessed enough to copy him."

"No!" Isaac insisted. He held his hands up as if to ward off the accusation. "I didn't do anything like that."

"No?" Paige said. She shifted tack quickly, because sometimes the surprise of doing so could catch a suspect off guard enough to get them to give up information before they intended to. "Tell us about why you were fired, Isaac. Tell us about the women you were harassing."

"That was all a misunderstanding," Isaac said.

"Was it?" Christopher asked. "Is that what the women will say when they're called as witnesses at your trial?"

Paige could see the fear renewed again on Isaac's face. "I didn't kill anyone!"

"No?" Paige asked. "Where were you last night? Where were you two nights ago?"

"I…," Isaac shook his head. "Nowhere, and you can't prove that I was."

Paige could see guilt written in every line of his posture. He was holding back, not willing to answer, and the reason seemed obvious.

"I think we'll find plenty of proof once we get warrants to search your home," Christopher said. "We'll go through your computers, through your entire life. And we'll take DNA. If there's one scrap of physical evidence at either of the crime scenes, you won't just be admiring Lars Ingram from afar, you'll be joining him on death row."

Isaac started to stand. "I didn't do this!"

"Sit down!" Christopher ordered him, obviously thinking that he was about to try to fight his way free.

The more Paige saw of his reactions, though, the less convinced she was that he was the killer. It wasn't the denials; every killer would do that as a matter of course. It was the fear, the suddenness of his reactions. Paige could see plenty of guilt there in his expression, but the more they asked him about this, the more Paige found herself believing that his guilt was about something else.

"What *did* you do, Isaac?" Paige asked. "What did you do that made you run from us? What did you do that has you jumping around, scared that we'll ask about it?"

"I'm not scared of you!" Isaac said. "Scared of a woman? When all you do is mess with people's heads, lead them on, get them fired?"

So he blamed the women he'd worked with for his firing? That wasn't entirely surprising, and it fit with the profile of someone who might go out and kill.

"You want to know why I went to see Lars Ingram?" Isaac snapped. "Because *he* knew how to deal with bitches who spent all their time pretending to care, but who were really just out for what they could get from people."

"But you still say that you didn't kill anyone?" Christopher asked.

Isaac gave him a determined look. "I didn't."

Christopher leaned over the table. "Why should we believe that? You still haven't told us where you were last night, or the night before."

Still, Isaac hesitated.

"What were you doing, Isaac?" Paige asked. "What were you doing that was so bad that you'd rather we thought you were a killer than talk about it?"

Isaac glared at her, sudden and direct. "I was following them! All right? Is that what you want to hear?"

"Who were you following?" Paige asked.

"Check my phone."

He took it out, putting it on the table and opening it up for them. He called up its photos, and they showed a woman in her twenties, young and pretty. The photographs showed her walking back from a bar, showed her heading towards a house, showed her through a couple of the windows as she moved around. They were exactly the kind of pictures the killer might have taken, except that the woman in those pictures was neither Marta Huarez nor Zoe Wells. Instead, Paige recognized the receptionist from the firm Isaac had been fired from.

Paige flicked through the photos there, checking for any sign of the two women who had been killed, but there wasn't anything.

"So you were stalking the receptionist from the place you were fired?" Paige said. "Why?"

"Because…" Isaac looked away now. "I wanted to kill her. I was *going* to kill her. I just…"

Paige realized what the shame was, then. "You couldn't do it. You wanted to, but you couldn't, and now you're ashamed that you're *not* a murderer?"

"I should have been strong!" Isaac said. "I should have been able to do everything that *he* did. But I didn't. I just sat outside her house, all night."

"*All* night?" Christopher asked. "You didn't go off anywhere else?"

Isaac shook his head. "I thought, if I just worked up to it…"

So his defense to the accusation that he'd murdered someone was that he'd been trying and failing to murder someone else?

"We can check the location data on your phone," Christopher said. "We'll know if you're lying."

"I'm not lying," Isaac said. "Look, I didn't hurt anyone."

No, he'd just stalked them instead. Paige looked over at Christopher who nodded and stood up, heading for the door, leaving him in there for now and taking the phone.

"We'll get the phone checked for his location last night," Christopher said. "The GPS data should still be on there. It should tell us if he's telling the truth."

"And if he is?" Paige asked. She suspected that he was, but she didn't like the idea of releasing a would-be killer back into the world. Maybe next time, he would find the impetus he needed to cross the line into murder.

"Then we still hold him on charges of stalking," Christopher said. "He needs to be off the streets before he hurts someone."

Paige appreciated his determination about that. They had a problem, though.

"If he *does* turn out to be innocent, then we have no more obvious suspects," Paige said. "Sorry. The whole point of having me along on this was that I was meant to be able to find the right suspects among Lars Ingram's visitors."

Christopher shook his head, though. "The point was that you're capable, resourceful, and you can get into the heads of killers. You're good at this, Paige, and there's no one I'd rather have along."

He put his hand on Paige's arm as he said it, and Paige had to remind herself that it was just a friendly gesture, not anything more. Christopher was a married man. There wouldn't be anything between them. There couldn't be. Especially not now that they were working together. The FBI had rules about that kind of thing, and Paige wasn't going to be the one to break them.

Especially when she had no real evidence that Christopher felt the same way. He was always friendly with her, and he obviously respected her as a psychologist, but as far as Paige knew, that was as far as it went. She wasn't going to risk trying to push things further.

Christopher stepped back. "Look, between the visit to Ingram and chasing down this creep, we've eaten up most of the day. We should call it a night, get some rest, and start again tomorrow. By then, we'll have the results back on Coleridge's phone, and if it isn't him, then hopefully we'll have thought of a way to make progress on the case.

Paige hoped so too, because otherwise, a killer was going to be out there still, free to kill again.

CHAPTER TWELVE

This was the first time that Amelie Pichou had been alone in the von Ryan family home since she'd come from Lyon to work for them, and it felt a little strange, being in such a huge place without anyone else there.

When she'd first come here, the idea had been to see a little more of the world. Getting paid while she studied just for looking after a couple of children had seemed easy. After all, she had four younger siblings back in France.

It had worked out well. The von Ryans were kind and generous, if busy in those strangely undefined ways that very wealthy people sometimes seemed to be. The children, Adam and Essie, were a delight, and as long as Amelie planned everything carefully, she still got to study.

When she wanted to see more of the sights around the city, she made it into a field trip for the children. A social life was more difficult, but she still got some nights off when the von Ryans were home.

And tonight, the house was hers.

Amelie wandered through it. A part of her wanted to throw a party, but she suspected that would lead to instant dismissal, however kind the von Ryans were.

She got herself a beer instead and started to cook herself a late supper. She could have ordered takeout, but honestly, Amelie had never gotten over what she knew was a very French aversion to American fast food.

There was food in the refrigerator, though, and the von Ryans had said before they left that she was welcome to any of it, since they would be on a skiing trip for a week, the kind of vacation that Amelie had never been able to take as a kid.

Being left behind was *her* vacation. Maybe tomorrow she would take a trip out somewhere beyond Washington, just to see more of the country she'd come to visit for a year. She couldn't be away for the whole week, because the von Ryans were leaving her there at least partly as a house sitter, but a day wouldn't hurt.

It wasn't as if the house needed the extra protection of one au pair at home. It had an elaborately sophisticated security system, with alarms and cameras that would pick up any intruder. It wasn't armed at the moment, obviously, because Amelie wanted to be able to move around the house without a private security firm breaking down the door, but once it was, this was probably just about the safest place it was possible to be. At night, it was even possible to arm just the downstairs alarms, making sure that everyone could sleep safe upstairs.

Amelie ate and then settled in to watch some TV, and this was one part of her job that she was somewhat grateful to have a break from. There were only so many cartoons she could watch with the kids before she needed to watch something more sophisticated.

It probably didn't help, though, that she chose to watch a horror movie. Maybe not the best choice when she was alone in a big house with the darkness closing in around her. It meant that Amelie jumped with every shock, and as the tension rose in the movie, she felt herself glancing around the living room, her eyes chasing imaginary horrors.

Deciding that maybe watching a movie like this wasn't the best idea, Amelie got up and turned the TV off, then went upstairs. She reached the top of the stairs, and went over to the alarm panel, ready to set the system and go off to her room. After the movie she'd just watched, she found that she wanted to feel secure, even if she wasn't going to go to sleep just yet. She still had some books to look over.

Amelie's hand was hovering over the keypad for the alarm when she heard a sound from downstairs.

Instantly, Amelie's head filled with thoughts of intruders breaking into the house, of burglars and home invasions, there because they'd heard that the von Ryans were away. The movie she'd just watched brought up other images: of some nameless horror creeping around downstairs. The ludicrousness of that thought made Amelie laugh to herself.

She knew what she ought to do. She ought to just set the alarm as she'd been intending, and if the sound downstairs was anything real, then help would be coming soon. Amelie could just hide in her room and let the professionals take care of it all.

If she weren't quite so creeped out by the movie right then, Amelie might have done just that. The trouble was that she wasn't entirely convinced that she'd actually heard anything. It *might* just be her imagination playing tricks on her thanks to the movie. If she set the alarm and went off to her room now, she would lie there in the dark, her imagination refusing to let her sleep.

It was nothing; she was sure of it. It was the effects of being in a dark house alone.

That meant that Amelie had to go downstairs to prove it to herself. She wasn't going to let herself be afraid of the dark. Even the children weren't scared of it. Determined to make sure that she could sleep tonight, Amelie went back downstairs, heading for the living room, where she thought the sound had come from.

Amelie was surprised to see that the TV was still on, the rest of the movie playing out in front of her. Had she not turned it off properly? Was that all this was? With a sigh, Amelie went to find the remote to turn it off again, and saw that it had fallen onto the floor, tumbling from the arm of the elegant, modernist chair it had been sitting on.

Amelie bent down to pick it up, and some flicker of movement made her stand up again in a hurry, spinning around to see a man standing there, dressed in black, a mask over his face so that his features were obscured.

Amelie just had enough time to see the flash of metal in his hand before he lashed out with the knife he held there, stabbing her.

Amelie screamed and fell, agony filling her. She clutched her stomach, and then the man was standing over her. She wanted to tell him that she was just the au pair, that she didn't have anything for him. She wanted to tell him that he could take anything he wanted from the house.

But then he was kneeling beside her, and Amelie could only watch in agonized terror as the knife rose again…

CHAPTER THIRTEEN

Paige was in the woods again, walking anxiously, looking for her father. The trees rose up around her, arching in ways that distorted the light, dappling it and turning it into a patchwork of shadows that meant she could never quite be sure about where she was putting her feet on the path.

That path stretched away in front of her, leading her on, step by step, even though she knew that she ought to hang back, to wait for the others. She wasn't meant to be out searching for her father like this, even if he was lost somewhere in the woods. She was meant to leave it to other people to find him. It wasn't her job, and it wasn't safe.

But she *was* his daughter, and as far as Paige was concerned, that made it essential for her to keep looking.

She stalked along the path, the trees seeming to curve in more tightly now, until every step Paige took was in half light. It was impossible to see the edge of the woods from here, and without a clear sense of the sun above, there was no way of knowing exactly which way she was going. Her father was the one who'd taught her to navigate using the sun, so that she would never truly be lost.

There were those who said that he'd just left them, just walked out on her and her mother, heading off into the woods, determined not to come back. Paige knew that wasn't true. Her father wasn't the kind of father who abandoned his family.

Paige kept searching, and as she did so, a sense of dread started to fill her. It wasn't just the surrounding trees, where the branches seemed to reach out like questing fingers, determined to grasp her.

No, it was because she knew what was waiting for her. She knew what she was going to find; she shouted at herself to turn back, but that didn't work. It couldn't work. She was no more than a passenger within herself, carried along by footsteps that fell exactly where they had always fallen, impossible to turn aside from their appointed route.

Paige saw the marker ahead, the one where she stepped off the path, searching through parts of the woods that she shouldn't have gone into. She was meant to stick to the paths in the woods, meant to stay in places she could find her way out of, but Paige knew with a grim certainty that she was going to step off, look deeper, even as she screamed at herself not to do it.

Some things were impossible to change, though, no matter how many times she'd seen them.

Paige stepped off the path, heading down past the great bulk of a fallen tree, looking around herself, trying to catch any glimpse of her father. This part of the woods led to one of their favorite spots, and Paige felt certain that if he was anywhere, he would be there.

At the same time, the deeper part of herself, the one that was forced to watch helplessly, knew *exactly* what she would find there.

A clearing lay ahead, beautiful with wildflowers, the sun breaking through in a way that it didn't in the rest of the woodland. Yet there was nothing warm or kind about the fall of the sunlight there. It was a harsh, almost clinical light, and Paige felt cold in spite of its presence as she stepped out.

There was a single tree in the middle of the clearing, and now Paige somehow saw two things simultaneously.

Her mother was there, tied to that tree, and her father was beneath it. The same spot, and both her parents, there.

Both of them were dead.

Her father lay at the base of the tree, the blood pouring out of him onto the soil beneath, carefully cut from him by precise wounds delivered by a scalpel. Her mother hung above, trapped in the web of ropes Adam Riker had tied her in, her body lifeless without a mark on it.

No, that wasn't what had happened. Her mother hadn't died. Paige had gotten there in time!

Yet here and now, her mother hung above her, while Paige ran to her father in horror, exactly the way her memory told her that she had before, trying to find some sign of life in him, trying to help. In life, he'd been so big and strong, so vibrant, so seemingly invincible; yet here, like this, he seemed pale and hollow, the ghostly pallor of his corpse staring up at her with empty eyes.

Paige knelt above him, and heard her voice calling out for help, again and again, until she was hoarse with it.

She heard someone coming. Her memory told her that people had come and found her, that soon Paige had found herself surrounded by cops and paramedics, taken away to an ambulance, asked questions that she couldn't begin to answer.

Now, though, she saw a shadowy figure on the edge of the trees. For a second, she thought that it might be Adam Riker, but it wasn't; this figure didn't look like him. This was someone else.

Instinctively, Paige knew that this was the man who had killed her father, and she was on her feet then, no longer a scared little girl, but someone who was training to be an FBI agent. Someone who wasn't going to back down. Someone who had a gun in her hand, ready to do whatever it took to stop him.

Paige ran after him through the trees, trying to keep him in sight while the branches whipped at her skin, hard enough to draw blood. Paige kept running, taking twists and turns, not slowing down even as the ground got rougher with fallen trees and tangled roots. Paige fell and got up again, keeping going.

The killer was in sight again now, just a few steps ahead. Paige fired at him, and saw splinters fly from a tree near his head. She fired and fired again, but the gun clicked empty, leaving Paige just sprinting after him, trying to close the distance.

She tackled the killer, sending the pair of them sprawling to the floor. She hit out at him, then dragged him over onto his back, determined to finally confront the man who had killed her father.

A blank face stared back at her, no features there to tell Paige who he was, no hint of his identity. Paige stared down at him and screamed out in a mixture of rage and horror.

She woke up in a cold sweat, sheets tangled around her. Paige could see the light streaming in through the window and checked her clock. Five am. Earlier than she would have wanted to get up, but there was no way that she was going to get back to sleep now.

She got up and got dressed, then went out into her kitchen area and got breakfast. Her thoughts wouldn't move away from her dream. The fact that her mother had almost been killed in the same spot where her father had been murdered lent a whole new layer of terror to the dream that had haunted her ever since she was a girl. Joining the FBI academy hadn't changed the core of the dream; it only added new elements to her chasing after the killer.

The faceless killer was always the worst part of it, because that was the part that still hurt when Paige woke up. She still missed her father, and still hated what had happened to him, but not knowing who had killed him was the worst part.

She went over to her bookcase, reaching between a couple of reference books to remove a box file and taking it over to sit at the small coffee table. With her usual research, Paige liked to keep the files on her computer, but not this. This was far too personal.

Slowly, she took out the old newspaper clippings, the fragments of reports that she'd been able to find, a couple of maps, several photographs, and her own notes made over several years. There were her notes on the few interviews with people she'd been able to get, using her PhD thesis as a cover to go and talk to them.

It meant that she had a lot of information, and Paige had read it over so many times that she knew the basics about this serial killer by heart. The Exsanguination Killer had been active for perhaps three years before he killed her father, although Paige knew that there was always the possibility of finding an older case somewhere further down the line.

To date, he seemed to have killed as many as fifteen people, mostly preferring men, although one woman had also been killed alongside a man, apparently when she had interrupted the kill and he hadn't been able to get away. The murders were big enough to make the news whenever they happened, and distinctive enough that they weren't likely to be mistaken for anything else, so Paige was fairly confident of the numbers.

His methods were consistent: he immobilized his targets using a stun gun, bound them, took them to a secluded location if they weren't in one already and then cut major veins so that they would bleed out slowly but surely. It seemed to be a point of pride for him to inflict the minimum of additional trauma with no major slashes or stabs to the bodies. All the wounds seemed to have been made with some kind of very thin, very sharp blade: probably a scalpel.

The majority of the murders had taken place in the open air, and the couple that had been indoors had taken place in secluded cabins out in the woods. This wasn't a man who was attacking targets in their homes.

Beyond that, Paige knew that she didn't have nearly enough information. There were limits to how much she had access to, even as a researcher into serial killers. She didn't have the full police files on the murders and had no idea if there was useful trace evidence that might allow her to finally find him. She guessed not, because the police might have found him by now if there was.

One she joined the FBI fully, she might be able to look closer. It was just one more reason to make sure that she completed her training successfully.

The Exsanguination Killer's last kill had been a couple of years ago. He'd been dormant since then. It was possible that some change in life circumstances had stopped him from killing or shifted his focus away from it. Some killers stopped temporarily while they were in relationships or in prison on some minor charge. Maybe the killer was even dead. For all Paige knew, he might have had a heart attack walking down the street.

As horrible a thought as it was, Paige hoped not. She hoped that this was only a temporary pause. She hoped that he would kill, or try to kill, again. It wasn't enough for her for the murders to stop. She had to know who had done this. She had to have answers.

Paige was still contemplating that when she heard a knock on her door, loud enough that she jumped. She couldn't imagine who would be there at this time of the morning.

She went over to the door, looking through the spyhole, and was surprised to find Christopher standing there, a worried look on his face. He raised his hand to knock again, and Paige pulled the door open.

"You're awake, that's good. I need you to get ready to go as quickly as possible."

"Why?" Paige asked. "What's happened?"

Something must have happened to bring him around here. She couldn't imagine him coming around just because he wanted to see her. Well, a part of Paige *could* imagine it, but she also knew that it wasn't ever going to happen.

"There's been another murder."

CHAPTER FOURTEEN

This crime scene was a lot fresher than the Estrom house. Perhaps it was the speed they drove there, but by the time Paige pulled up at the door with Christopher, the first news vans were barely starting to arrive, and the CSI crews were only just moving in.

"How long ago was this called in?" Paige asked Christopher.

"Less than a half hour. An au pair working for a wealthy family. I came to get you as soon as I heard."

A murder had been reported, and Christopher's first instinct had been to come get her? Did he really think that much of her ability to help him with this case? Paige was both grateful for that and a little intimidated, because of what it implied if she wasn't the one to come up with answers on this case.

"Let the CSI team go in first," Christopher said. "We don't want to contaminate the crime scene any further than it has been by the local cops who were here first."

They waited, plastic suited crime scene techs moving in ahead of them. Paige could see the TV crews setting up around the edges of the property, cameras already starting to point their way.

"We'll check the perimeter," Christopher said. "The local cops have cordoned it off, but I want to see if there's any sign of how the perpetrator got in."

Paige walked around the garden with him, checking the flower beds around the edge of the property.

"Here," Christopher called out, pointing to a spot in the beds. A couple of the crime scene investigators started to hurry over.

Paige saw what he was looking at: a smudged half footprint sat there in the flower bed. Paige guessed that it could have been from a gardener or someone else who worked there, but it was tempting to believe that it was from the killer jumping over the fence.

"You see there?" Christopher said, as the CSI team moved in to take photographs. "That alley across the street? If he came over the fence here, my guess is that he came in through there. We'll have to check down that way for cameras that might have caught sight of him approaching."

Paige was impressed by how much he'd gotten from one mark in the dirt. It seemed that he wasn't done, though.

"Look at that camera. It's been disabled, and it covers a side door. The killer found a way to get in without being seen," Christopher said.

Which meant that he'd planned all of this carefully, and that he had the skills to take out a camera without being spotted.

They went over to that door. It was unlocked.

"Either someone inside forgot to lock this…" Christopher began.

"… or the killer picked the lock," Paige finished for him, which suggested that the killer had at least some basic skills when it came to breaking and entering.

"Exactly. We should be able to head inside now." Christopher passed Paige a pair of latex gloves to put on. Rather than going in through the side, though, they headed around towards the front door of the house, presumably to avoid trampling on any part of the scene that the CSI unit hadn't gotten to yet.

"Agent Marriott!" a reporter called out from the edge of the property. "Can you tell us what the FBI is doing here?"

Christopher ignored him, so Paige was determined to do the same.

"Can you tell us what Dr. Paige King is doing here? Is this linked to Adam Riker?"

Paige felt a flash of tension at that. She could remember the other times reporters had been shouting questions at her all too well. They'd delved into every detail of her past in the last case. She didn't want their attention now.

She and Christopher went inside without providing any of the answers that the reporters wanted.

This house was pretty much the opposite of the Estrom house: bright and ultra-modern, minimalist and decorated in whites and grays, built probably no more than ten years ago. Yet it shared a sense of wealth with the Estrom house, larger by far than most suburban houses would have been, the banks of windows giving a broad view out over the city, the few ornaments looking as though they probably cost more than Paige's car had.

The crime scene techs were there, moving over it carefully, checking every inch of the place for physical evidence.

"The body is in the living room," one of them said as Paige and Christopher made their way through the place. "Just through there."

Paige saw Christopher nod and steeled herself as she stepped into the living room. Even so, it was hard not to be shocked by the sight of a young woman lying face down there on the floor of the room, stripped wood floor around her stained darker with blood, blonde hair pooled around her like a second spill. Paige suspected that it would be almost inhuman not to feel the wave of horror that stole over her at the sight of the young woman there.

Forensic investigators crowded around the body.

"What do we have, Lamar?" he asked one of them, a middle-aged Black man with a short beard whose bulky frame filled out the blue plastic of the evidence suit he wore. He seemed to be running things here, which said to Paige that he had to be with the coroner's office.

"Our initial information says that this is Amelie Pichou," the other man said. "Twenty years old. Died sometime last night." He looked over at Paige. "Who's this?"

"This is Paige King," Christopher said. "She's working with me on this. Paige, this is Lamar Smithson, with the coroner's office here in D.C. If there's anything to find out about a body, he'll manage it."

"But *not* so soon after arriving," Lamar said. "We're only just getting ready to turn the body." He looked around at a cluster of other techs. "On three. One, two, three."

They turned the young woman onto her back, so that she stared up at Paige with unseeing eyes. She would have been pretty in life, but in death, her features had taken on a hardness that seemed almost accusing.

"Ok, initial impressions suggest that this is a young woman who died late last night, possibly in the early hours of this morning. Certainly not within the last couple of hours, or there wouldn't be the kind of lividity we're seeing here. I can't give you an official cause of death, but I'm seeing multiple stab wounds."

"Seven?" Paige said, before she could stop herself.

"*That* is something I won't be able to determine until the autopsy," Lamar replied, with a note of reproach. "I see that you have the same kind of impatience Agent Marriott usually exhibits."

Paige felt a hint of embarrassment at that rebuke, but when she looked across at Christopher, he shrugged.

"Don't mind Lamar. He never wants to commit to anything until he's sure he's examined every speck of evidence."

"Anything else is just guesswork," the coroner said.

Paige didn't want to imagine what he might think of her role in all of this, then, trying to get into the head of the criminal behind all of this.

"Was Amelie alone here in the house?" she asked Christopher.

He nodded. "She was house-sitting while her employers took a vacation in St Moritz with their children."

"So how do we even know about the murder?"

Christopher looked momentarily impressed, and Paige was glad that she'd done something he thought was good.

"It turns out that her employers had a live feed from a camera above the TV. Ms. Helen von Ryan saw the body and reported the death."

Paige tried to imagine what that would have been like for Helen von Ryan. She knew firsthand how awful it could be finding a body, having been the one to find her father's, but to spot one over a camera, unable to do anything about it… in some ways, that was even worse.

"My office has arranged to speak to her when we've taken a look at the house. For the moment, though, I want to check the security here."

Christopher led the way out of the room, up through the house, to a spot where an alarm keypad sat on the wall. It was blinking green, suggesting that it had power.

"The alarm wasn't disabled," he said.

"Meaning that Amelie didn't have a chance to arm it?" Paige asked.

"Exactly. I think we have enough to talk to Helen von Ryan. We'll go through to the kitchen and do it there."

He led the way down through the house, to a bright, modern kitchen complete with breakfast bar. They sat at that while Christopher got out his phone and made a call.

"Yes, this is Agent Marriot. I'm ready to FaceTime with Helen von Ryan, if you can get her. Thanks."

Paige was slightly impressed by the fact that Christopher could just make a call to have that kind of thing arranged for him. It was a reminder that he was just one part of the bigger machine that was the FBI. That they *both* were, even if she wasn't entirely official yet.

It wasn't long before a call came through to Christopher's phone. He answered it, and a woman's face appeared on screen. She was probably in her forties, with dark hair and brown eyes, looking utterly stressed out and nervous to Paige, her hair in disarray, her hands moving constantly, her eyes darting around.

"Ms. von Ryan?" Christopher said. "I'm Agent Marriott, with the FBI. This is my consultant, Dr. Paige King. I know this must be hard for you, but if it's possible, we'd like you to answer a few questions for us."

Paige saw Ms. von Ryan hesitate, but then nod.

"Yes, yes, of course. Eddie is with the children, but all of this… it's such a shock, I'm sorry."

"You were the one who made the report about the murder?" Christopher said.

"Yes, that's right. I… we have a webcam set up, letting us keep an eye on the property while we're away. I checked in on it, and I saw… I saw… Amelie was just lying there. I didn't know what to do. I ended up calling the police here, but of course I don't speak much French or German, and it took *forever* to explain to them what was going on."

"And they contacted us," Christopher said.

"Ms. von Ryan," Paige asked. "Amelie was your au pair?"

"Yes, that's… Oh God, how am I going to break this to the children?"

An au pair definitely fit the serial killer's pattern, but Paige wanted to know more.

"And when was it decided that she wouldn't accompany you on vacation? I guess a lot of people might have taken their au pair to look after the children while they skied."

Ms. von Ryan seemed a little caught by surprise by that question. "We made the decision a few weeks ago. We thought it would be a nice break for Amelie, and since Eddie and I aren't at work, looking after the children isn't an issue. If we'd just taken her with us…"

"You couldn't have known," Paige said. But the killer had known. He'd planned this in advance. He'd known that last night, Amelie Pichou would be alone in the house. "Tell me, did you talk about your vacation on social media?"

"Well, yes," Ms. von Ryan said. "I was so excited to take the children away skiing like this, and we weren't worried about burglars seeing the post because Amelie was staying home. Plus, we have a state-of-the-art security system."

Which hadn't been switched on, and so hadn't slowed the killer down at all.

Christopher took over the questioning again then. "Ms. von Ryan, when you were looking at the camera, did you see anything out of place? Anything that wouldn't normally have been in your living room?"

"Just Amelie, with her lying there, and the blood…"

It was obvious that Amelie's employer was in shock after everything she'd seen. Paige doubted that after what she'd seen, she would have picked up any details at all, no matter how unusual they seemed.

Christopher obviously felt the same way.

"Is it possible that we could get access to the footage from the webcam?" he asked.

"We... didn't set it to record," Ms. von Ryan said. "I only glanced in out of curiosity. Recording everything would have felt as though we didn't *trust* Amelie."

So they were mistrustful enough to watch her, but not enough to record what was happening? That was frustrating to Paige, because it meant that one potentially crucial piece of evidence simply didn't exist. The camera could have given them their first real look at the killer, but instead, they had nothing.

"Thank you for your time, Ms. von Ryan," Christopher said. "You've been very helpful. If you remember any details at all, please, don't hesitate to get in touch."

Paige couldn't help feeling a surge of disappointment as he hung up. Maybe they would get some evidence from the crime scene, but the killer's previous murders suggested that he was more careful than that. Even if they did, it would take time, and this killer seemed to be acting much faster than Lars Ingram ever had. It meant that Paige and Christopher had to come up with another way to find him, and fast.

CHAPTER FIFTEEN

They drove back to Christopher's office, and Paige used the time to think about how they were going to make progress in finding the copycat. She knew that Christopher was relying on her. Maybe some physical evidence would come through on this, but she suspected that what they really needed was for her to find some insight, some link, that they could go on.

"Do you think that there's a link between the three murders beyond them all being of young women involved in caring for people?" Paige asked Christopher, as they pulled into the FBI parking lot.

"Would there have to be?" he replied. "You're the expert on this, Paige."

The expert. It was another reminder of just how much they all needed her to be the one to come up with something in the current absence of physical evidence.

Paige shrugged. "I'm not sure. With Lars Ingram, that was enough for him to select his victims. He seems to have done it randomly, looking out on the street or online for women who met his criteria, then following them until he was sure he would be able to kill them without being caught."

"So our guy could be doing the same," Christopher said, in a grim tone. He obviously knew as well as Paige did that, in that case, it would be harder to catch him.

"He could," Paige admitted. "But it's also possible that he's deviated from what Ingram did in this. Some copycats copy a killer's methods, but then apply them to a group of victims that has more meaning to them, more of a connection. I know it's a long shot, but if there *is* a link between our victims, that might lead us back to our killer."

Christopher seemed to consider it for a moment or two, and then nodded. "It's worth looking into. You start running background checks on the victims; I want to chase any possible camera footage from along the route the killer must have taken, and keep on top of the CSI results as they come in."

Meaning that there would be a lot of responsibility on Paige's shoulders. She would effectively be working alone, trying to collate every scrap of information that she could about Marta Huarez, Zoe Wells and Amelie Pichou. It was potentially daunting, but it was also familiar in a way. She was used to sitting alone, trying to do in-depth research. It was just that, previously, lives hadn't been at stake.

"He's going to kill again," Paige said, as the two of them got out of the car, starting to head up to Christopher's office.

"Not if we stop him," Christopher replied. "Besides, we might get lucky. It might just be those three he wants dead."

That didn't sound like good luck to Paige, not when three women were already dead. In any case, she didn't think it was likely.

"Serial killers don't just stop. Sometimes life events stop them, or sometimes they pause between kills, but that isn't likely in this case. We have a pattern of escalation here that suggests he's going to try to kill at least one person a day."

"Unless we catch him," Christopher said.

Ultimately, that was what it came down to. The two of them had to catch this killer, or he would continue to murder young women. Three had died already at his hands, but if they got this wrong, then other women would die too.

That thought fueled Paige as they reached Christopher's office. She started to look up the three victims using DMV records, tax records, internet searches and searches run through the FBI's databases.

In the modern world, there was plenty on all three, although perhaps not as much as Paige might have expected from people their age. The social media profiles for the three women were there, but they didn't spend as much time posting on them as a lot of women in their twenties might have. They certainly didn't spend a lot of time posting about the exciting places they'd been, or about the big nights out they'd had. The time they'd spent caring for others had seemed to leave no room for their own lives.

Maybe that was a part of the killer's motive.

"Is it possible that the killer is murdering these women because he's saying that they've already given up most of their lives to care for others?" Paige mused aloud.

Christopher was looking through files on his computer.

"It's possible, although I'm not sure if that helps us get closer to identifying him."

"And I guess there's the problem of whose motive we're dealing with," Paige said.

Christopher looked over at her, obviously waiting for her to explain.

"What I mean is that our copycat doesn't *have* to have a motive of his own beyond really liking Lars Ingram's work," Paige explained. "Maybe Ingram killed for the reasons I just described, but this new killer might not share the same motives."

"So it might not get us anywhere?" Christopher asked.

Paige shook her head. "Sorry."

"No, it's good to work through all of this, and try to work out what's relevant. I've been checking for cameras along the route the killer must have used to get close to the house. Sadly, there doesn't seem to be anything close enough for us to be sure that anyone we see on it is the killer."

Paige understood. A figure glimpsed close by just before a murder was almost certainly a suspect. One spotted half a mile away ten minutes beforehand could easily just be someone out for a nighttime walk, with no real way to link them to the crime.

Paige just hoped that she would be able to come up with something that was more helpful, and soon.

The trouble was that the victims didn't seem to have that much in common beyond their age and their choice of profession. If those were really the only ways the killer was choosing his victims, then there was no real link back to him, no thread that they could follow that might end at his doorstep.

Then a thought hit Paige.

"Wait, it's not about *why* he's selecting his victims; it's about *how*. His motives don't matter right now, but it does matter where he's going to spot his victims."

Any point of connection between Marta, Zoe and Amelie might show where the killer had first spotted the three of them. Once they had that, then they had somewhere they could start looking for answers.

The difficulty lay in finding that point of connection, because the three of them didn't seem to have very much in common, based on a combination of what Paige could find in the files and what was available to look up about the women. Marta Huarez had been a part of a big, bustling family, while Zoe Wells didn't really have anyone, and Amelie Pichou's family was back in France. Their workplaces were entirely separate, and they didn't seem to have any friends in common on social media. As for socializing, Paige wasn't sure that they even got any time to do that, but the few references she could find to it in Marta and Zoe's profiles didn't have any obvious locations in common. It wasn't as if all the overnight caretakers went to drink in one bar together.

Paige felt certain that there had to be something, though. It seemed that Christopher did too.

"You're looking for a connection between them?" he asked.

"If we find that, we might find where the killer first picked them out as potential targets," Paige said.

"Ok," Christopher said. "I'm going to make a couple of calls to try to see if anyone close to them heard one of them mention the others. Sometimes, with something like this, it can be that simple."

Paige nodded, and watched as he flicked through a notebook, obviously looking for the relevant phone numbers. It meant that she didn't have to do it, and that she could keep her focus on the information in front of her, trying to make some sense of all of it.

"Hello, is that Marta Huarez's sister? This is Agent Christopher Marriott, with the FBI. I'm looking into your sister's death... Yes, that's right. I know this must be very hard for you. I had a question about your sister that I hoped you might be able to answer for me. Did she ever mention women named Zoe Wells or Amelie Pichou to you? In any context? I'm trying to establish if she knew them. Please, take your time. You're sure? Well, thank you for your time."

Paige knew without asking that Christopher hadn't had any luck with the first call, but her attention was firmly on trying to think of other ways that the three women might have some kind of connection. It occurred to her then that, if the killer was trying to target women working in caring professions, then the point of connection for the three of them was likely to be something to do with their work. Paige tried to think. How did people get jobs like that? She guessed that some applied to vacancies directly, but it was much more likely that they applied through an agency.

Paige looked through the files on the first couple of victims, searching for any reference to the agencies that had gotten them the job. She found what she was looking for in Zoe Wells's financial details: she got paid through something called the Sunshine Care Agency.

"Are you about to call the von Ryans?" Paige asked Christopher.

He nodded.

"Can you ask them if they found Amelie through an agency?"

79

"You think you've found something?"

"Not yet, but people working in their field often work through agencies, right? And if I wanted to find details about a lot of women doing that kind of work as a killer, then maybe an agency would be the place to start."

She could see how that caught Christopher's interest. "I'll check."

While he was doing that, Paige decided that she wanted to check up on Lars Ingram's victims. They were two separate cases, but was it possible that the copycat had copied, not just Ingram's method of killing, but also his approach to finding victims?

Paige didn't know, but she was determined to find out. She called up the files on the Ingram case, looking back through the financial details of the victims, which seemed to have been included in the files as a matter of course. With most of them, there was nothing direct, but in two more cases, Paige saw references to the Sunshine Care Agency.

By the time she was done, Christopher was getting off the phone. Paige looked over at him expectantly.

"Yes, they used an agency to hire her, one based here in D.C."

"Did you get a name for it?" Paige asked.

"The Sunshine Care Agency."

Suddenly, Paige could feel excitement building in her. "That's also the name of the agency Zoe Wells was hired through, and a couple of Lars Ingram's victims."

She searched for the agency, and pulled up a glossy web page, promising to find highly trained care staff *For All Your Care Needs.*

"That might not mean anything. I mean, Ingram's cases are separate."

"Not if this killer learned about how he found some of his victims and decided to copy that part too," Paige said.

Christopher was starting to look a little more convinced, but it still obviously wasn't absolute.

"Was Marta Huarez hired through them?" he asked.

Paige shook her head. "But that might not mean anything. With a lot of these places, people go on the books of several agencies. Maybe Marta sent them her resume but got her job a different way before they found her anything. There are a lot of ways for an employment agency to be aware of people without actually finding them a job."

Resumes, connections to other agencies, lists of potential workers built up through contacts to maybe poach away later for different jobs.

An agency might have plenty of people on its books who didn't get their current job through them directly.

"It's possible," Christopher conceded, "and we don't have much else to go on right now until the forensic reports come back."

"They have an address in D.C.," Paige said, looking over the website. "It's not that far."

"Then we'll go there," Christopher replied. "And maybe we'll be able to find out how our killer is finding his victims once we're there."

CHAPTER SIXTEEN

As he and Paige pulled up outside, Christopher had to admit that the Sunshine Care Agency wasn't quite what he expected of it. The offices were bright and shiny, upmarket and clearly aimed at attracting an expensive clientele, but were in a neighborhood that was a little rundown and grubby.

Christopher guessed that most of the clients didn't go there in person; they would arrange everything in a call or two and find the staff member they needed within a day or two. Yet they obviously wanted the place to look good just in case anyone *did* drop in to find staff personally.

He and Paige went up to the agency and stepped inside. They quickly found themselves greeted by a young male receptionist with a bright smile and spectacles. He was dressed in a dark suit that might have been better suited to someone working at an investment firm, he and seemed polished to an almost improbable degree.

"Hello," he said. "Can I help you? Are you looking for someone to care for an older relative, or perhaps for your child?"

Christopher felt a flicker of embarrassment at the assumption that he and Paige were a couple. He found his thoughts flickering to Justine, his wife. They'd talked about having children before, but they both led such busy lives. If they ever did have children, would they need an au pair to let them handle everything? Would Christopher still be able to run around chasing after serial killers?

"We're not a couple," Christopher said, taking out his ID to show the receptionist. "I'm Agent Marriott, and this is Dr. Paige King. We'd like to speak to a manager, about Zoe Wells and Amelie Pichou."

He could see from the shock on the receptionist's face that he'd heard those names on the news and understood what this was about.

"If… if you'll just wait here for a moment," he said, and hurried off into the rest of the place, leaving Christopher and Paige standing there in front of the reception desk.

"I can't believe he thought that we were a couple," Christopher said, looking around at Paige. "Sorry. I should have cut him off before he got to that."

"No, it's fine," Paige said, but she seemed slightly flushed, as if embarrassed by it all. Of course she was; she was only just starting out in the FBI, and was probably determined to be taken seriously as a professional. Christopher wanted to make this all as easy as possible for her.

A prim woman in her fifties came out to the desk, dressed in a dark skirt suit, with her dark hair tied back, and a discrete silver necklace strung around her throat.

"Hello. I'm Madeline Evans, the manager here. Please, come through to my office."

She hurried them through the main offices of the firm, past several desks where people were working at computers or making calls, presumably to place more care staff in suitable positions with absolute discretion.

Ms. Evans led the way through to an office that was furnished in modern style, with a wide glass table to hold her computer screen and a large leather office chair set behind it. There was a wide white leather couch on one wall, with a smaller table set in front of it. Christopher guessed that it was for client meetings, and it was there that the manager of the Sunshine Care Agency led them.

"What can I do for you, Agents?" she asked as they sat down.

"Have you heard the news about the recent murders?" Christopher asked. "Marta Huarez, Zoe Wells, Amelie Pichou?"

He watched her face as he said the names, trying to see if there was any hint of recognition there in response to them.

"I'm sorry, I don't understand what that has to do with us here," Ms. Evans said. "What do murders have to do with us?"

Christopher looked over to Paige, letting her take this moment.

"Amelie Pichou and Zoe Wells both found the jobs they were doing at the time of their deaths through your agency," Paige said. "So did Linda McCarthy and Tammy Khorikian. Those two were murdered by a serial killer named Lars Ingram."

"A serial killer?" Ms. Evans said. Now Christopher could see the horror and fear on her face. "I really don't understand. If you know who this killer is…"

"We believe that another killer is copying his work," Christopher explained. "We also believe that he might be using your agency as a way to locate his victims."

"But that… that would mean…"

"Someone who works in the agency, or at least who has access to your files," Paige said.

Again, Christopher saw a look of horror cross the manager's features.

"No, that can't be right," Ms. Evans said. "It's simply not possible that someone here would do something like that. We wouldn't hire a *killer*."

She made it sound as if they would just put it on their resume for everyone to see. As if it were obvious just from looking at people whether they were killers or not.

Christopher suspected that the hardest part of this wasn't going to be getting information out of this woman; it was going to be convincing her that her agency could ever have had anything to do with all of this.

"We're not saying that any of this is your fault," Paige said. "But you *do* have the chance to help us now."

"Help you how?" Ms. Evans said.

"Can you tell us how all of this works?" Paige asked. "How does someone go about getting a job through you, and how do people end up with particular people working for them?"

Ms. Evans gave a bright, professional smile then. Evidently, this was something that she was more than happy to talk about and had probably explained to people plenty of times. If it got her to relax enough to answer more questions, then it was definitely a good place to start.

"All our workers begin by sending in a resume," Ms. Evans said. "They then go through an extensive vetting process, making sure that no one we employ is a criminal or has any skeletons lurking in their past."

Which was fine, unless they simply hadn't been caught for what they'd done, or unless they started it after they began to work at the agency. Even the best checks couldn't guarantee that a serial killer wasn't working there.

"We also interview them to find out the kind of work they wish to do, and the kind of environment that would best suit them," Ms. Evans said. "Above all, we look for people who will truly *care* about the people for whom they will provide support."

"And once you've determined that they are suitable?" Paige asked. "How do they get matched up with specific jobs?"

84

"People put in a call to us with the details of the position that they want filled. Then one of our agents goes through the files of the people they have on their books and finds a suitable match."

"Presumably you keep records," Christopher said. "Records of who found jobs for which people?"

"Yes, of course, it helps us to work out their bonuses at the end of the year, and to make sure that each of our recruitment agents is hitting their targets."

She made it sound so brisk and efficient, a long way from the caring approach that she had been so proud of just a few moments before. At the same time, though, the most important thing was that they *did* have those records. If they could show a connection between the murdered women and a single individual, then whoever that was would rocket to the top of their list of suspects.

"We'll need to see those records," Christopher said. "Plus any information you have on people who sent in resumes but weren't found jobs."

"I'm really not sure," Ms. Evans said. "We pride ourselves on our discretion. It's one of our major selling points with our wealthier clients. If we were to simply give out information, it might look very bad for us."

"It would look worse if people heard that you could have helped to catch a killer, but decided not to," Christopher pointed out.

"And I'm sure you want to find the person who has been killing people employed through your agency as much as anyone does," Paige suggested, taking a much more conciliatory tone. "It's not about discretion, Madeline. It's about doing the right thing. I'm sure the people who employed Amelie and Zoe would want to know that you're doing everything you can to try to find the person who killed them."

The good cop, bad cop combination seemed to be enough for Ms. Evans, because she nodded.

"Yes, yes of course. I wouldn't want anyone to think that I wasn't helping."

She led them around to her computer screen and called up a spreadsheet.

"Here, this is our record of who is employed where, which agent got them the job, what they're being paid, and what percentage is due to our agency under the terms of their contract. If you give me a moment, I should be able to find the names. Remind me of them again?"

"Amelie Pichou, Zoe Wells, Linda McCarthy, Tammy Khorikian," Paige supplied. "I'd also like you to check Marta Huarez's name to see if she has any connection to your agency."

It seemed to take forever for Ms. Evans to check the names, calling the relevant sections of the spreadsheet up on the screen. Christopher looked over her shoulder, and immediately saw one issue.

"It seems that the women were all placed in their positions by different agents," Ms. Evans said. A strange look came over her face, as if she'd just thought of something, but she seemed to compose her expression into something more precisely professional. "So you see, it seems impossible that one of my employees would have had contact with all of them. I'm sorry, but you've wasted your time here."

It sounded like a dismissal. Christopher knew that he ought to have felt as though the bottom had dropped out of this lead, if not the entire investigation. Yet there was something about the speed with which the woman seemed to be trying to get rid of him and Paige that made him suspicious.

"What are you holding back?" he asked.

"I don't know what you mean," Ms. Evans said.

"You thought of something before," Christopher said. "There was something, just as you told me that they were all put in place by different agents."

"It's nothing," she said. "Just a suspicion."

"Even that might help us a lot," Paige said. "Whatever you've thought of, the more information we have, the better."

Christopher heard Ms. Evans sigh. "There was a man who worked here. Ben Astor. I believe that Zoe Wells made a complaint about him. That complaint crossed my desk."

"What was the complaint?" Paige asked. "What did she accuse him of?"

Ms. Evans sat there for a moment, either trying to remember or trying to work out how to phrase it.

"He got her personal information from our files," she said at last. "He used it to contact her outside of the scope of her employment. He sent her messages that were… well, entirely inappropriate, trying to get a date with her. When several other young women also made complaints about his behavior, I had no choice but to let him go."

"When?" Christopher asked.

"A couple of months ago."

But not before he'd worked at the agency for more than long enough to do damage, with full access to the personal details of young women. If this man was their killer, then his time at the agency would have given him a whole storehouse of potential victims, along with the details of exactly where to find them in their jobs.

"I need an address and a phone number for him, please," Christopher said.

It meant one thing in Christopher's mind: they had a suspect at last. They needed to talk to Ben Astor as soon as possible.

CHAPTER SEVENTEEN

To Paige, Ben Astor's home looked more suited to a small family than to a single recruitment consultant. It stood in the suburbs, amid rows of other houses that had the same square, identically built look to them. It had a small patch of lawn out front, a driveway with enough room for a couple of cars, and a neatly trimmed hedge dividing it from its neighbors. There was no car in the driveway, but that didn't necessarily mean anything.

It seemed quiet, peaceful, and not at all the kind of place where a serial killer might live. Yet the more Paige thought about Ben Astor, the stronger a possibility he appeared to be the copycat killer.

He had access to the files for Zoe Wells and Amelie Pichou. It seemed entirely possible that he might have been able to find details for Marta Huarez somewhere else, perhaps from a resume sent in to him but not logged into the system, perhaps from an online job board somewhere.

He was undoubtedly a creep as well, just based on the reasons he'd been fired from the recruitment agency. There was no doubt that he'd used the information he had in inappropriate ways.

Maybe being rejected and fired had been what pushed him into killing. Maybe he'd gotten angry, looked around, and seen Lars Ingram's work. Maybe he'd decided that copying it was exactly what he needed right then.

It was a lot of maybes, but as they got ready to walk up to the house, Paige felt confident that they would be able to find answers here, one way or another.

She and Christopher walked up to the front door. Christopher hammered on it, the two of them waiting there in silence, listening to see if there was any response from inside the house.

It was silent. There was certainly no sign of anyone coming to the door. Did that mean that Astor was out, or that he was hiding, having worked out that they were law enforcement? No one watching them walk up would have mistaken Paige and Christopher for anything other than FBI.

"I'm going to check around the back," Christopher said. He didn't add 'in case he makes a run for it,' but Paige knew that was what it had to be. Paige watched Christopher go and realized that she was basically guarding the front door now. If Astor suddenly came bursting out, she was the one who was going to have to slow him down or stop him.

Christopher was trusting her to do that, and Paige just hoped that she would be able to remember enough of her training to deal with it if necessary. She wasn't a helpless grad student anymore. She was most of the way, well, *some* of the way, to being a trained FBI agent.

Paige was still waiting out there when she saw a man come out of the house next door. He was in his fifties, balding, wearing slacks and a cardigan.

"Excuse me," he said. "What exactly do you and your friend think you're doing, wandering around someone else's property? I'll call the police."

It occurred to Paige that maybe it wasn't obvious to *everyone* that she and Christopher were with the FBI. It seemed that, to Ben Astor's neighbor, they looked like they were casing the property, getting ready to burgle it. She guessed that she should just be grateful that this was the kind of quiet suburban place where people came out and threatened to call the police, rather than rushing out guns blazing to deal with the threat.

"We're with the FBI," Paige said. "My partner is an agent, and I'm…" What was she now? A trainee? Certainly not a full-blown profiler yet. "…consulting with him on a case. We need to speak to Ben Astor urgently."

It seemed that Paige managed to inject the right note of authority into her voice to be believed, because the neighbor's expression changed almost instantly from one of stern confrontation to something far more helpful.

"You won't find him here. He didn't come home last night."

"You're certain of that?" Paige asked.

"I keep a very close eye on the neighborhood, looking out for my neighbors, making sure that there isn't any trouble."

He made being a nosy neighbor sound practically like a public service. In this case, though, it was potentially useful.

"So Mr. Astor didn't come home last night," Paige repeated.

"Not for several nights, in fact," his neighbor said. "Oh, has something happened to him? Is that why you're here? Do you think he's in some kind of danger?"

"No, we don't have any reason to believe that right now," Paige said. But right then, she *did* have plenty of reasons to think that Ben Astor might be their guy. Mysteriously gone at night, right on the nights when the murders had been taking place?

Christopher came around the corner. "There's no sign of him at home."

"He isn't here," Paige said. "His neighbor here was just explaining to me how he hasn't come home at night for the last few nights."

She could see that Christopher understood the importance of that instantly.

"Thank you for your assistance, sir," he said to the neighbor, and gestured for Paige to head back to the car with him. "We need to find him, now."

Paige nodded. "The only question is how. If he's not at home, and he's been fired from work... wait, I have an idea. We have a phone number for him, right? Could we trace that to find his location?"

"Potentially," Christopher said. "Although to be completely precise, it's better if we have him on the phone for a while."

"I can keep him talking," Paige promised. She already knew how to play this. "Just set up the trace."

"Hold on," Christopher said, and took out his phone, making a call. "Yes, this is Agent Marriott. I'm going to need a trace on a number my associate will be calling. Yes, I'll wait... right, thank you. I'll text you her number now."

Christopher nodded to Paige. "The techs are ready. Make the call and keep him talking so that they have time to narrow it down."

Paige called the number they'd been given for Ben Astor. It rang a few times, and Paige was worried that it would just go through to voicemail, but then, thankfully, someone picked up.

"Hello?" a male voice said.

"Hello, Mr. Astor. My name is Paige. I was given your number by a friend who said that you helped her to get a job working as an overnight caretaker for an older lady. I hope you don't mind me calling, but I hoped you might be able to help me to find something similar."

There was a brief pause on the other end of the line. "I guess that I might be able to help," Astor said, "but this isn't the best time. I'm kind of in the middle of something."

What did that mean? Given everything Paige suspected about him, she was terrified that it might mean that he was getting ready for another murder.

"This won't take very long though," Paige said. "I just wanted to tell you about my passion for caring, and maybe about the kind of client that I'm hoping you can find for me."

"I'll be happy to discuss it later, but for now, I really do have to hang up," Astor said. The phone clicked into silence a moment or two later.

Paige looked over at Christopher, worried that she hadn't managed to do enough. If Astor really was on the verge of killing someone, and they didn't find him, then another woman might die. All because she hadn't managed to keep him on the phone long enough.

Christopher smiled, though, as he looked up from his phone. "The techs were able to hack into the GPS signal for the phone. They've sent over the address. We have a location for Ben Astor."

"We need to get over there, now," Paige said.

They drove over, and as they did, Paige did her best to look up the location they were heading to. She wanted to know where Astor was, and what he was doing there. While Christopher drove, weaving in and out of the traffic at speed, Paige typed the address into her laptop, and found the name of the owner: Lisa Handel.

Paige looked her up as quickly as she could, and even the most basic of searches revealed a fact that made her blood run cold.

"Lisa Handel, the owner of the apartment we tracked the phone to? She works as a private nurse for an older couple. She's exactly the kind of target our copycat likes. He's going to kill her, Christopher."

In that moment, Paige was convinced that they'd found their man, and that worse, he was already getting ready to kill again. If he was in Lisa Handel's building, then he had to be at least scouting the area, if not actively in the process of trying to kill her. They had no more time to lose.

Thankfully, Christopher seemed to feel the same way, because they were driving along at speed now, lights flashing to keep cars out of the way. They skidded to a halt outside an apartment building, and Paige was already rushing out of the car as it came to a stop.

"It might be safer if you stay here," Christopher said, getting out.

"No way," Paige said. "I'm training to be an agent. That means I don't just sit in the car and let you walk into danger alone."

Christopher looked as though he might argue, but with so little time, there was nothing he could do but nod. "All right, but you stay behind me."

They rushed into the apartment building, then up the stairs, heading for the apartment Ben Astor was in. Reaching it, they paused outside the door. Christopher had his gun out now, his expression set.

There was no question of knocking, not when that might spark Astor to finish his kill. Instead, Christopher kicked the door, breaking it open in one movement that sent splinters flying.

They plunged into the apartment together, and Paige saw a woman there, heard her scream in horror. A man who could only be Astor stood across from her. He was tall, in his early thirties, clean shaven, with short blond hair and a silver stud in one ear.

"Get your hands in the air Astor!" Christopher ordered. "Do it now!"

The woman screamed again. She was a little taller than Paige, slender, with dark hair. She was wearing a floral print dress and looked completely terrified.

"What did you do to my door?" she cried out.

As she said that, Paige started to get the feeling that something was very wrong here, and not just because of Lisa Handel's reaction. There was also the fact that Astor was just standing there, in plain view, with no weapon in his hand. Then there was the way he kept glancing across to Lisa, not like he wanted to kill her; more like he wanted to make sure that she was ok.

"What is all this?" Astor demanded. "Who are you?"

"FBI," Christopher said. "Don't move. We know about what you've been doing."

"What I've been doing?"

He sounded genuinely confused.

"Christopher," Paige said, starting to understand. "Look at them. Ms. Handel, are you safe? Did this man try to harm you?"

She looked both confused and frightened then. "No, of course not. Why would Ben do anything to hurt me?"

"Ben?" Christopher said. "You know him?"

"Of *course* I know him," Lisa said. "He's my boyfriend."

Paige felt all the adrenaline that had been coursing through her until that moment run out of her in a rush, leaving her feeling suddenly empty and embarrassed. She'd thought that they were chasing down a killer, but they'd actually only found out that Astor's tactic of reaching out to young women on his company's books had finally worked for him.

"Where have you been for the last three nights?" Paige asked him. "Your neighbor says that you weren't at home."

"I was here, of course," he said.

Paige looked over at Lisa Handel, who nodded.

"He was with me. Look, will one of you tell us what's going on?"

What was going on was that they'd gotten it wrong. *Paige* had gotten it wrong. She'd leapt to the conclusion that Ben Astor might be their killer, and the moment there had been a fragment of evidence that supported that, she and Christopher had gone blundering in to try to capture him. Yes, they'd done it because they thought that a woman's life was in danger, but they'd still smashed their way into her apartment and pointed a gun at her boyfriend.

Ben Astor wasn't their killer. They were back to the start on this case, again.

CHAPTER EIGHTEEN

Paige sat in Christopher's car feeling embarrassed and dejected as they drove back towards the FBI building. She'd messed up, and because of that they'd broken their way into a woman's home with weapons raised. She'd jumped to conclusions and gotten this wrong.

"Don't be too hard on yourself," Christopher said, obviously catching sight of her expression.

"I don't think I'm being hard enough," Paige said. She sighed. "Honestly, Christopher, I'm starting to worry that you should have a real profiler with you, not someone half trained."

"There was enough of a connection to Ben Astor for him to be a suspect, and once you worked out what Lisa Handel did for a living, even I thought that she was in danger," Christopher replied. "My guess is that any of the profilers I could have been teamed up with might have come to the same conclusions."

"But it wasn't them," Paige said. "It was me. I messed up. I'm not sure that I deserve to be here."

That was hard for her to say, because she wanted to be there, more than anything. It wasn't just that it was the job that she wanted to do more than anything, it was the fact that she was partnered with Christopher, getting to work with him up close and bounce ideas off him.

"Well, I know you do, or I wouldn't have requested your help," Christopher said. "Look, I could drop you back at the academy if you really want me to, but that would leave me without a partner on this, and also eat up time we don't have. Besides, I *want* you working on this, Paige. Now, are you going to keep going?"

A part of Paige still felt as though she ought to give up, but she pushed that part down. If she really wanted to work in the FBI, then she couldn't afford to give up like that. If she went back to the academy now, her instructors would ask the reason why, and when she told them, she was sure that they would never feel comfortable about letting her out into the field. Agents didn't get to pick and choose whether they kept going with cases, and even if she wasn't an agent yet, neither could Paige.

"I will," Paige said. "But I'm not sure what we need to do next."

"We keep working the leads we have until we can find another," Christopher said.

So far, they'd looked at two main leads. They'd tried to get Lars Ingram to give them information, and they'd looked at the Sunshine Care Agency.

"I want to go back to speak to Lars Ingram," Paige said. "I want to try to get him to talk."

She'd struck out before, but maybe now that he'd had time to think, he might be more inclined to answer her questions, especially if she thought of a new way to persuade him.

"He's scheduled for execution tonight," Christopher said. "And you heard him yesterday. He isn't going to help us without getting something in return. We'd be wasting our time talking to him."

"I have to try," Paige said. "If I *can* get any answers out of him, I think it has the potential to blow this case wide open."

If his copycat had gotten in touch, even briefly, then Lars Ingram might have the answer they sought about his identity.

Christopher's expression was thoughtful. "Possibly, but I still don't think that we can use all our time trying to get a psychopath to talk. I want to go back to the recruitment agency, and check each of their employees. I think there's still a chance that the connection you found there could turn out to be more, and I don't want to let it go just yet."

"You don't need me for that part," Paige said. Yes, she could be an extra pair of hands looking into the recruitment agency, but she would be more helpful trying to make use of her training and the time she'd spent working with the worst killers, trying to get some answers out of Lars Ingram.

"You still want to go to the prison?" Christopher said. "Alone?"

"I spent half my PhD talking alone with killers," Paige said. "I'll be fine."

"All right. I'll drop you at your place, and you can drive over from there. I'll let them know that you're coming. Just... promise me that you'll be careful."

*

For the second time in as many days, Paige found herself walking through death row, escorted by a guard, going to see a serial killer. She could feel the pressure of the eyes on her from all sides, and tried to move carefully, keeping well away from the cells on either side as she went to the visiting room.

Paige sat there on one side of the table, separated from the rest of the room by the plastic screen. The dull gray surroundings of the room felt much more oppressive without Christopher there beside her. It both reminded her, and didn't remind her, of the build up to her therapy sessions with Adam Riker, back at the institute. There was the same sense of anticipation, bordering on fear, that came with knowing that she was about to match wits with a serial killer. There was the same sense of needing to get information out of someone dangerous, who would only engage with her on his own terms.

There were differences, though. The room was a long way from the comfortable, soothing environment of the institute. Where that was designed to be calming, this place was simply designed to contain until the prisoners there could meet their inevitable fate.

The biggest difference, though, was that Paige didn't have the same confidence that she'd had talking with Adam Riker. With him, she'd thought that she was getting all the information that she wanted smoothly, through her own cleverness; yet she'd learned the hard way that he was playing his own game, controlling what he told Paige while getting more information than he gave.

Memories of her interactions with Adam left Paige on edge as she waited for Lars Ingram to arrive. She knew the stakes here: the copycat killer would keep murdering young women until he was stopped, and she remained convinced that one of the best ways to do that was to try to get information out of the serial killer he was copying.

Doing that meant sitting there and waiting while a guard fetched Lars Ingram. He shuffled in wearing his manacles, and if he was afraid about this being his last day on earth, he didn't show it. Instead, he merely looked annoyed by the interruption to his day of Paige being there.

"Coming alone this time?" he said, as the guard fastened him into place. "I don't even warrant two of you now?"

"Or maybe I think that you're worth my full attention," Paige suggested. "Maybe I don't want us to be distracted while we talk."

"I've got nothing to talk about with you," Ingram said.

The guard moved to stand in the corner of the room, but Paige waved him away. "Wait outside, please."

It took all of her nerve to say that. Once, back at the institute, she might have insisted upon it as a matter of course, wanting to get results that weren't influenced by the observer effect of having a guard there watching every interaction she had with a patient. Now, after Adam Riker had escaped, threatening Paige and her mother, it was much harder to do.

She had to do it, though, if she was going to get answers.

The guard went reluctantly, shutting the door behind himself.

"Determined to show me how brave you are?" Ingram asked.

"Do you prefer women to be scared around you, Lars?" Paige shot back. She wasn't just going to come out and ask him for help this time. That obviously wasn't the way to get anything out of him.

He shrugged. "I prefer them to die."

It was terrifying, the nonchalant way he said that: a reminder that this was a genuine psychopath, one who truly didn't care when it came to others, maybe even didn't view them as real.

"But only ones who are taking care of someone else?" Paige asked. It was important to build up to the real questions slowly, working their way around to them, trying to build trust. "Why them, Lars. Who hurt you to make you want to hurt them?"

"You think you can understand me that easily?" he snapped back. "You think I killed them because… what? Some babysitter abused me when I was a kid?"

"Did they?" Paige asked.

"You want to know the real reason?" Ingram said. "Because they're *weak*. They spend their time following around after old people who should be left to die. They spend their time pretending that they care, taking the money."

"So it's a sense of justice that motivates you?" Paige asked.

Ingram smiled at her across the table. "Is this where you ask me to help you to catch the killer you're chasing out of a sense of justice?"

His tone made it clear that he wasn't going to give her an answer just because of that, so Paige backed away from that approach.

"No. I'm interested in you."

There was no doubt that Lars Ingram would only be interested in himself. It was just a question of finding a bridge to the things that Paige actually wanted to know.

"Are you?" he said. "What, are you planning to write a book about me?"

"My PhD was on serial killers," Paige said. "Maybe I *will* write about you. But for that, I'd need information."

"All about what made me into me?" Lars Ingram said. He gave her a look of almost snarling hatred, lunging forward to the limits of the cuffs that held him in place so that Paige jumped back in spite of herself. Ingram laughed then, long and loud, obviously enjoying her discomfort. "You don't know half of what I've done."

"There's a pretty well documented list of the people you killed," Paige pointed out.

"That? They didn't get close to the reality. You're still trying to work out why I did it? Maybe I just discovered that I liked doing it. Maybe I just found that I was good at violence, that I enjoyed it. Have *you* ever killed anyone, Miss FBI?"

Paige found herself thinking back to the moment when she'd been standing over Adam Riker, holding Christopher's gun. When he'd been taunting her, trying to get her to finish him. She could remember the part of her that had held back, and the freedom that had come from knowing that she didn't have to be as bad as him, just out of some sense of revenge.

"No," Paige admitted, "I haven't."

"What was that look?" Ingram asked, and Paige could see that she'd caught his interest.

She knew that she should tell him, then, tell him exactly what had happened with Adam. But hadn't that been exactly the mistake she'd made with Adam? She'd given up information, thinking that it couldn't hurt, and it had, more than she could have imagined.

"I haven't killed anyone," she repeated.

"Ah, but you've wanted to, or you came close. You should have. Maybe then you'd understand what it's like." There was a note of contempt in Lars Ingram's voice. "You can't understand the pure satisfaction at the moment of the kill, the knowledge that you're just *better* than someone."

"Do you think that's what your copycat feels?" Paige asked, trying to steer it back around to what she wanted to know. "Do you think he feels everything you feel, or are you better than him too?"

"Is *that* your play to get me to talk?" Ingram asked. "You're going to try to make me so jealous of this guy that I just blurt out anything I know about him. Well, maybe I know something and maybe I don't, but you won't get me to tell it to you that easily."

"What *would* it take to get that information?" Paige asked. Not that she had anything real to offer him.

"Come to my execution, and maybe I'll tell you something there," Ingram said. "I'd like to see just how squeamish you are when it comes to death."

Paige knew in that moment that he was just playing games with her, trying to waste as much of her time as possible. She had no wish to go to his execution and doubted that she would get anything useful even if she did.

"We're done here," she said, getting up and going to the door to call for the guard. Paige tried to hide her disappointment as she did so. She'd failed here, gotten nothing useful.

She just had to hope that when she got back to the FBI offices, Christopher would have had more luck with his lead.

CHAPTER NINETEEN

As soon as Paige walked back into Christopher's office, she could see that he didn't have anything that was going to blow the case wide open. He was pacing too much, looking too intently through the files, and there wasn't the expression of triumph on his face that there might have been if he'd managed to find something that would actually lead to the killer.

Paige was surprised that she'd learned to read his expressions so well. Had she really spent that much time looking his way? She knew that she must have, and even though she tried to tell herself that it was just because Christopher was someone she'd been in life-or-death situations with, she knew that it was more than that.

Except that it couldn't be; Paige had to remind herself very firmly of that.

"How did things go at the prison?" Christopher asked, as he turned and saw her entering the room. "Are you ok?"

Paige shook her head. "I'm fine, but I didn't get anything out of Ingram. I got the feeling that he just wanted to play games and boast about how we didn't know half of what he'd done. He said that if I came to his execution, he might tell me something then, but that's just him playing another game."

Christopher seemed to think for a moment or two. "I agree. I don't think we're going to get anything out of following the Ingram lead further. Are you sure you're ok? I realized when you were gone that this would be your first time talking to a killer alone since…"

"Since Adam," Paige said. "I know. And yes, it brought up some stuff, but it didn't stop me from doing my job."

"I never thought it would," Christopher said. "I was just worried."

Paige shrugged. "I'm ok. Or I will be, once we actually catch this copycat killer. How did things go at the recruitment agency?"

The fact that Christopher hadn't come out and shouted about some further lead that he'd found supported the idea that there wasn't anything, but Paige still asked, hoping that she was wrong, and that he'd at least found something that they might be able to turn into more with further work.

"I looked at everyone who works there," Christopher said. "None of them seem like suspects. They all have alibis for at least one of the last three nights, and there's nothing in their pasts to suggest that they might be the kind of person who would do this. I also checked to see if Marta Huarez had so much as sent in a resume, even if it was rejected. As far as I can tell, she didn't."

Which made it unlikely that the killer was finding his victims through the recruitment agency. It meant that the connection Paige had thought she'd found was just coincidence after all. The idea that they'd spent most of a day running around after leads that had turned out not to be relevant was a frustrating one. It meant that the killer just had that much more time in which to plan his next murder.

"Is there anything on the forensics?" Paige asked. She knew that she was there to help with the profiling side of things, but she found herself hoping then that some fragment of forensic evidence would give her the spark she needed to help Christopher find this killer.

"I'm reading through the preliminary reports now," Christopher said. "Although some things will take longer in the labs to confirm. At the moment, it looks as though there aren't any unexpected prints at any of the crime scenes, and no DNA that we picked up at the Amelie Pichou scene matches any that we have on file."

Meaning that they weren't going to catch the killer with a convenient strand of hair or ungloved hand at the scene. Paige could feel Christopher's frustration at the lack of physical evidence, or maybe it was just her own frustration at the answer not being simple, when this killer was likely to strike again soon.

"The lack of evidence tells us that he's careful," Paige said. "There's also maybe something to the part where he's targeted victims in a couple of wealthy homes."

"He didn't take anything, though," Christopher pointed out, "so I doubt that this is about the money. And Zoe Wells was killed in a retirement home. An upscale one, sure, but still not a fancy house."

"I don't think it's about the money," Paige said. "But maybe there's a part of it that's about the challenge? Wealthier homes are more likely to have high tech alarm systems, and the retirement home had cameras he had to avoid."

Of course, that was all just conjecture, and Christopher seemed to know that too.

"We have no real way of knowing for sure," he said. "And even if we did, then I'm not sure that it would help us to find him. At most, it helps us to narrow down his list of future targets."

The worst part was that, at the moment, that seemed to be all they were left with: trying to narrow down the list of future targets in the hope that they could keep them safe. That gave Paige another potential piece of the puzzle.

"Maybe that's a part of it too," she said. "This isn't a group where we can give them all protection, or even ask them to stay home for a few days while we solve this. We can't ask them to leave town for a while like we did with some of the people that we thought Adam Riker was going to target, because then other lives would be at risk."

Paige realized that insight wasn't any more helpful than the last one had been.

"Sorry. I should be able to give you more than this."

"Can you tell me something about the kind of person this is likely to be?" Christopher asked. "That might help us get closer to working out who he is."

Paige nodded. That much, she could do. "I can give you a few basics, and maybe a few general guesses based on what we've seen of the crimes so far."

She watched Christopher sit down behind his desk, opening up his computer, and Paige realized that he was actually preparing to take notes. It felt so strange, with her observations being taken that seriously by someone in the middle of catching a killer. Yes, she'd done assessments on criminals at the institute, and she'd helped out with the first case, so it wasn't as if she was entirely unused to being listened to, but it still made for a big change from writing a PhD thesis that was destined to be read by maybe a dozen people if she was lucky.

Paige took a seat opposite Christopher, trying to gather her thoughts.

"We used to think that the most likely profile for a serial killer was a white male in his mid to late twenties, possibly of above average intelligence," she said. "Some of the more recent analyses of people who have killed more than once suggests that almost none of that is necessarily true for the US. Yes, serial killers are overwhelmingly male, but only 52% are white, and a mere 27% fall into that mid to late twenties age range." Paige realized the way she was setting it out. "Sorry, I'm lecturing."

"No, it's fine," Christopher said. "I asked, after all."

"Having said that, 27 is the median age at which male serial killers make their first kills, so if these are this killer's first murders, he may actually fit the classic age range. His home life is likely to have been disruptive, but the idea that all serial killers come from broken homes and suffer abuse is false."

So far, it was just general information. Paige did her best to be more specific.

"This one's fixation on Lars Ingram is significant. Probably he heard about Ingram's crimes at some particularly important moment for him psychologically, and then researched him in order to find out more. It might be possible to track that research if it was done too openly, but honestly, all of Ingram's crimes are well known, so enough research on the internet might give him everything..."

Paige trailed off as she thought about what Ingram had said to her back at the prison.

"What is it, Paige?" Christopher asked her.

"There's something that Lars Ingram said when I went to see him," Paige explained. "It seemed like an idle boast at the time, but now it has me wondering. He said that people didn't know half of what he'd done. I thought he was just trying to be as frightening as possible, but what if he meant it more literally? What if he killed more victims than we think he did?"

"He was convicted for more than enough as it is," Christopher said. "And he's due to be executed for those crimes later today. I'm not sure what difference it makes if he committed more murders, at least as far as this case goes."

"I don't know," Paige said, "but it feels connected to the rest, somehow. I want to at least check."

"I guess we don't have anything else to go on right now," Christopher said. He sat with his fingers poised above his computer keyboard. "What are we looking for?"

"Any other murder that might plausibly have been his," Paige said.

"So any murder around the period we know that Lars Ingram was active?" Christopher said.

"Plus possible missing persons," Paige replied. She knew without being told that it would be a large number, but they had to find a way to narrow it down. "But not all of them. We're not looking for kids who have run away and come back a few hours later, or ones who have obviously gone off to try to make it in LA."

"Presumably, we're looking for women in their twenties," Christopher said.

"Specifically, ones who worked as caretakers, nurses, that kind of thing." Paige didn't think that was a part of Lars Ingram's MO that he would be willing to compromise on.

"That *does* narrow it down a little for the last three or four years," Christopher said. His tone had changed to something more intent, apparently seeing that they might be able to get something out of this now that they were able to narrow it down.

Paige went around to his side of the desk so that she could see the computer better, standing behind Christopher as he flicked through the files. She tried to work out which ones might be relevant.

"This one was looked at before," Christopher said. "Andrea Wilson. But the police at the time didn't think that the MO of the crime fit the pattern, because she was killed outdoors."

"I think we should include it on the list," Paige said.

They kept looking, trying to find nurses and overnight caretakers, babysitters and au pairs.

Another case caught Paige's attention: that of a babysitter called Nikki Ashenko, who had gone missing almost three years ago. Technically, it was a missing persons case, because no body had ever been found, but she'd gone missing one evening in the middle of looking after two children. There were other possibilities too: a nurse who had just disappeared a year ago, a caretaker who had been killed at night, but it had only been a single stab wound, not consistent with Lars Ingram's method of stabbing people seven times.

"There have been serial killers before who claimed to kill many more people than the official count," Paige said. "The Zodiac Killer, for example."

"So you're saying that Lars Ingram might have killed all of these people?" Christopher said.

"Maybe," Paige said. "Or maybe our copycat killed some of them. And as professional as he is now, I bet he wasn't as neat or as careful the first time that he killed someone. If we can identify when that was, maybe we'll be able to find the evidence that we haven't been able to find at the scenes in the last couple of days."

Of course, to do that, first they had to work out if any or all of these new cases really were Lars Ingram's work.

CHAPTER TWENTY

Paige knew that she needed to see how these cases fit together. She needed to visualize the pattern in them, and that meant getting their details somewhere more physical than a computer screen.

She gestured to the glass board on one side of the room. "I want to construct a timeline, to see if it tells us anything. I need to see this."

"Sure," Christopher said. "What are you hoping to find?"

"I want to look at patterns of activity, to see if any cases stand out as potentially the work of our copycat."

Serial killers often had patterns to the timing of their kills. Those patterns could accelerate, but large deviations for no reason were rarer. If Paige could find one of those, maybe it would indicate a case that wasn't Lars Ingram's.

Paige drew a line on the board with a marker, then put in the most recent murders as a starting point, writing the dates and names in red. Those were a known starting point, murders they knew were definitely down to the copycat.

"Ok," she said, going back to the computer and checking the dates of the murders Lars Ingram was convicted of. She wrote those on the board in green, the kills stretching back three years, with fifteen women that they knew about dead in that time. Already, the intervals between the murders looked messy to her, but she wasn't sure if that was just normal variability in the data or something else.

Paige kept going, pulling up the missing persons files that seemed even vaguely suspicious and starting to add those dates and names in blue.

"Doesn't this just confuse things?" Christopher asked. "It's going to be hard to see real patterns when there are so many dates, and we don't even know which ones might be relevant."

Paige shook her head. "We need the data. The more, the better, right now."

She went to write Nikki Ashenko's name in, went back to the computer, and checked the date again. She frowned and wrote it on the board, drawing a ring around it and the murder that sat directly above.

"April 19th," Paige said.

"What about it?" Christopher said.

Paige pointed at the board. "Lars Ingram killed someone on April 19th, three years ago: Bethany Deering. Nikki Ashenko went missing on the same day."

"Meaning that Ingram couldn't have killed her," Christopher said.

"He physically might have been able to, but he's never committed two separate murders on the same day."

Paige could see Christopher looking thoughtful now. "Strictly speaking, we don't know that Nikki Ashenko *was* murdered. She just went missing. And even if she *was* killed, we don't know that it's related to any of the rest of this."

Paige could understand his caution, but she still thought that this was their best shot of getting answers in this case. She also thought that there were plenty of reasons why they *should* assume that this disappearance was connected.

"She was a babysitter, who went missing at night, while two kids were asleep upstairs," Paige said. "If she were going to run away somewhere, I don't think she would have abandoned the children to do it. She was early twenties, in a caring profession... she fits the profile."

"Ok, I'll agree that it looks pretty good," Christopher said. "But we would still need to find evidence that she was murdered before we could link it to the rest of this."

"Did the police search?" Paige asked.

"The file says they conducted a preliminary search but wrote it off as a runaway."

"Then I think we should check out the area of the disappearance," Paige said. "We have to know for sure, one way or the other."

For a moment, Paige thought that Christopher might not agree, but then he nodded sharply. "It's our best shot. Let's go."

*

They drove out to a small town in Virginia, the kind of place that Paige had grown up in. The kind of place where people assumed that everyone knew one another and that things were simply safer. Her own life had proven that wasn't the case.

Paige didn't know this particular small town, but she *felt* as if she did. It had the same kind of general store on the main street, the same cluster of small restaurants that wanted to pull in people from D.C. but mostly just catered to the locals. The same small gas station and collection of small stores that had probably been run by the same people for years.

They drove up to a small house on the edge of the town, where Nikki had been working when she disappeared. It seemed like a perfectly ordinary family home, backing onto a small stretch of woodland, with a single Citroen on the driveway and rose bushes in the garden.

Paige took a copy of the case file with her as she and Christopher went up to knock on the front door. A woman in her forties answered. She was round featured and dark haired, with a slightly harassed look, as if she'd been trying to do too many things at once before the two of them arrived.

"Hello?" she said.

Christopher held out his ID. "I'm Agent Marriott, with the FBI. This is my associate, Dr. Paige King. Mrs. Trenton?"

Paige saw the woman's expression go from harassed to worried, but there was also a note of understanding there.

"This is about Nikki, isn't it? The FBI coming all the way out here, it can only be about one thing. Have you found her?"

Paige shook her head. "We haven't. We were hoping that we could ask you what happened that night."

Mrs. Trenton's expression took on a pained look.

"I hoped that you might be able to tell me," she said. "Arthur and I were going out to dinner in the city. We got her to look after the children, the way she did a dozen times before. Then, when we got back, she was simply... gone. No note, no explanation. The children were asleep, so they couldn't tell us what had happened, either."

All of that fit with the report, and Paige didn't think that they were going to get much more out of this woman or her family.

"Did Nikki ever talk about wanting to leave?" Christopher asked, obviously trying to establish if there were any reasons to think that this might just be a missing persons case. "About having a new boyfriend, maybe, or about having dreams that would mean going somewhere else?"

"No, not at all," Mrs. Trenton said. "That was a part of what made it all so strange. She was happy here. She didn't have any reason to leave, in spite of what the local police thought."

That was very different from the reports at the time. Those had assumed that this was just a missing young woman. Paige was increasingly suspicious that it was more than that.

"Thank you for your time," she said. "Is it all right if we take a look around the area?"

"Yes, of course," Mrs. Trenton said. "You're welcome to come in and look around too. Although I don't know what you'll find now that all this time has passed."

Paige wasn't sure either, but she felt that she and Christopher had to try. She tried to put herself into the head of the missing young woman; tried to work out what might have happened.

She looked over to Christopher and stepped away a little so that the two of them could talk. "Assume for a moment that she didn't run away, because there's no reason to think that she did."

Christopher nodded. "That seems a reasonable enough assumption."

"Ok, so what if it *was* our copycat? We know he likes to break into houses."

"But he leaves the bodies there," Christopher pointed out.

"But what if Nikki *heard* him? What if she spotted him trying to ambush her? What would she do then?"

"Call the cops, probably," Christopher said. He didn't have to say that there was no record of such a call in the file.

"Only if she had enough time," Paige said. "The cops are great if you can hide in a room somewhere and wait for them, but what if he was too close for that?"

"She might have tried to fight, or run," Christopher said. His voice said that he understood where this was going.

"I think that she would have run," Paige said. "She saw a strange man in the house, and she would have thought about the danger the children were in. She would have tried to lead him away. She could have tried to run for one of the other houses, but since no one saw anything, my guess is that she went the other way."

Paige looked towards the woods.

"I guess she could have tried to lose him in there," Christopher said. "Although I'm pretty sure the local cops would have at least walked through that woodland to check for her before they wrote the whole thing off."

"I still want to look," Paige said. "If they weren't really looking, they may have missed something."

Christopher looked a little doubtful. "After so much time, it's possible we won't find anything."

"It's our best shot."

"True."

Together, they walked over to the patch of woodland. By day, it had a pleasant feel to it, the warmth of the sun cut through the shade of the trees and wildflowers there around their bases. At night, though? With someone chasing? Paige guessed that it would have been a terrifying place.

As Paige walked, she looked around, trying to spot any signs that might point to a shallow grave or a hidden body. At this point, as horrific as the thought was, her every instinct told her that Nikki Ashenko had been killed.

They reached a small stream, and Christopher spread his hands. "What now?"

Paige got out the file, reading. "It says here that on the night Nikki Ashenko went missing, it was raining heavily, which sounds like another reason they gave up so quickly. My guess is that even if they had searched, any clues would have been washed away."

Washed away. Those two words stuck in Paige's mind, refusing to dislodge.

"There was heavy rain," she repeated. "That might mean that a stream like this might flood. It would be flowing faster... we need to check downstream."

It would explain why there hadn't been anything to find in the woods, because the stream might have carried Nikki Ashenko clear of them. Then, when the water receded in the morning, the police would see the stream and think it was too slow and meandering to be relevant.

Paige set off along the bank of the river, heading downstream, searching as she went for any sign that might point to what had happened that night. Christopher went with her, but he clearly wasn't as convinced as she was.

"I know you're following your instincts on this, Paige, and I trust them, but this feels like a bit of a long shot. We have a lot of assumptions piling up on one another to get us here."

"I know," Paige said, "but I really believe this is what might have happened."

That seemed to be enough for Christopher. "All right, we'll keep going."

They walked along the bank of the stream together, and it might have been pleasant, if not for the reason that they were doing it. Both of them kept their eyes down, checking the stream and its banks, not wanting to miss anything.

They walked until they were well clear of the woods, and there was still no sign of anything. They must have gone at least a mile, now.

"I think we need to call this," Christopher said. "Even with a flood, there's no way that the stream could have-"

"Wait," Paige exclaimed as she spotted something on the bed of the stream. "What's that?"

Something shone white there, and as Paige hurried forward to get a better view, she realized with a sickening feeling that it was the top half of a skull. Horror started to fill her, and for a second or two, she might have been back in the forest, staring down at her dead father, but there was also excitement mixed in with it that she'd found the one thing they needed to keep going.

They'd found Nikki Ashenko's body. A killer had indeed murdered her on the night she'd gone missing, a night when Lars Ingram had been busy committing a *different* murder. This was the work of someone else, and if it proved to be the work of the copycat, then it might be a step closer to finding him.

A fresh wave of horror hit her at that thought. If Paige was right about all of this, then that meant that the copycat had been working for *years*.

The trick now was working out which other murders were the work of the copycat, and exactly how much Lars Ingram knew about him. As much as Paige hated it, there was only one way she was going to be able to do that.

CHAPTER TWENTY ONE

He sat at home, in his study, looking out over the peaceful suburban surroundings outside his home with a strange, almost disjointed contempt. How could the rest of the world live like that? How could they pretend that their lives were normal? How could people just drift from one banal moment of existence to the next?

How would they react if they knew that he was planning a murder even while they went about their drab lives?

Probably, they would be horrified. There was a time when he might have pretended to be too, when he had spent all his time trying to pass for normal. It had almost killed him. Now, *he* was the one who did the killing.

He'd been working quickly in the last few days, quicker than he normally would have. Normally, he left time between each kill, letting the impact of it settle in, making sure it was seen by the one person who mattered. Now, though, with Lars Ingram's execution scheduled for today, he had to move quicker.

Lars had been... an inspiration. More than that. Hearing about Lars had literally saved his life. Trying to fit in had made him depressed, had made him want to kill himself rather than live one more moment of the ordinary life that so many people seemed to settle for. He hadn't seen the point in going on if that was all there was.

He'd actually planned it. He'd decided that he would throw himself off a bridge into the Potomac, leaving behind nothing but a note. Even that seemed dull and empty now, a conventional way out of an all too conventional life.

Then he'd happened to look at the news, just killing time while he tried to summon up the courage to actually do it. A story about the latest murder by the Caretaker Killer had been there on the news, back in the early days when Lars only had two or three kills that anyone knew about.

That one moment had changed things forever. It was as if something had clicked into place inside him, showing him that this was what he was meant to do. He'd gone out and researched everything there was to find on the murders then. They were a template for him, a guide on how to be everything that the hidden part of him had always wanted to be and not get caught.

Two weeks later, he made his first kill, a babysitter out somewhere in Virginia. He was still a little embarrassed by how sloppy that one had been. He hadn't gotten the details right, and she'd managed to run out of the house before he could kill her. He'd caught up to her, though, and the exhilaration of the moment when he stabbed her had been like nothing he'd ever experienced before in his life.

That had been special, but in a lot of ways, the one he was planning now would be even *more* special, more meaningful, simply because of what it would represent. It wouldn't be his final kill, of course, he had no plans to stop. But it would be a particularly significant landmark.

After his first kill, he'd come to see himself as Lars Ingram's shadow. He'd realized that any kill he made would be attributed to the Caretaker Killer, but it had also become something of an unspoken competition between them. Whenever he'd seen a new kill by his idol, his *rival*, he would start to plot one of his own, trying to make it at least as spectacular, at least as difficult.

He wanted to show that he wasn't just some second-rate tribute act; he was an equal, a colleague, possibly the only other person out there who might understand. It didn't matter to him that the police thought that both sets of kills were the work of one man. If anything, that was simply validation that he was copying Ingram's methods perfectly.

He knew that Ingram started to respond to him. The rate of his kills went up, and there were whole phases where the two of them had seemed to be in a back-and-forth game of one upmanship, as if determined to have the last word. It had only stopped because the media and the police seemed to be so poor at picking up on the kills that belonged to the two of them. Fewer than half of the total murders seemed to actually have been labeled as Lars Ingram's work, and when Lars had been convicted, it had been for a random sampling of both their crimes.

It had been… disappointing when Lars had gotten caught, partly because it had shown that Lars wasn't perfect, but mostly because it meant that it was impossible to go on killing in the same way without it being obvious that there was a second killer at work.

He'd briefly considered changing his methods, but that hadn't felt right somehow. Instead, he'd stopped for a time, telling himself that he had achieved enough, ignoring the itch at the back of his mind. He'd watched as Lars was tried, convicted, and sentenced to death, the way someone else might watch seeing a sports hero brought low by injury. It had felt like the end of a dream.

As the execution loomed, though, he'd found the need to kill again proving harder and harder to ignore. Finally, he'd realized what his mind was trying to tell him: that he wasn't done, not even close. That there was something far more important he could be doing.

So he'd started his current spree, still in a game of one-upmanship with Lars, except now, Lars couldn't hit back with murders of his own. It finally gave him a chance to not just compete with, but actually surpass, his idol.

Yes, the world would see him, when before he'd been hidden, but that didn't have to be a bad thing. He'd found himself looking at the news reports with a kind of satisfaction that came from knowing no one was confusing his work with Lars's anymore.

One slight irritation was that they were calling him a copycat, as if he were merely second-rate. Still, after what he had planned, they would stop that soon enough. They would go from calling him a copycat to what he truly was: a successor.

Today, the Caretaker Killer would be executed, and tonight, people would see that his replacement was every bit as deadly.

CHAPTER TWENTY TWO

Paige had never been to an execution before, and she'd never had any desire to witness one. Her instinct, even when it came to killers, was to try to contain and understand them, not to kill them out of some need for vengeance. It was why she hadn't been able to pull the trigger when she'd had Adam helpless in front of her.

But now, it seemed, she and Christopher *had* to attend an execution.

"Are you sure this is a good idea?" he asked as the two of them arrived at the prison, walking through the small crowd of death penalty protesters who stood outside. Even with a man like Ingram, there were people who didn't like the idea of him being killed.

"We need to be here," Paige said.

"You came away last time convinced that Ingram was just playing games with you."

Paige nodded. "I know, but he also threw out the request for me to be at his execution as a kind of challenge. If I *meet* that challenge, if I actually show up, he might be impressed enough to tell us something."

"There's always a chance that he doesn't know anything," Christopher pointed out. "I mean, how many serial killers actually know their copycats?"

Paige could see that he had a point there, but in this case, she thought it was an increasingly likely possibility. "This isn't just a copycat; this is someone who has been killing almost as long. He's more like a partner, or a rival. It's entirely possible that the two made contact at some point, if not while Ingram was killing, then once he was in jail."

"We went through the call records, remember?" Christopher pointed out.

Paige nodded. "True, but I still think it's possible. At the very least, Ingram can tell us which kills are his, and which aren't. A final chance to set the record straight."

That was the part Paige suspected that he might jump at. She had no illusions now about any part of Lars Ingram wanting to do the right thing, or even hating his rival enough to give him up, but she suspected that his ego might be big enough to make him want to be clear about exactly what he had and hadn't done. *That* would make it possible to go through all the crimes that were definitely the copycat killer's, trying to find some common thread that would lead to him.

The two of them went into the prison, and at the reception desk, Christopher held up his ID. "We're here for Lars Ingram's execution."

"Take a seat, and a guard will lead you through," the receptionist said.

They sat there waiting, and Paige could feel her nerves building, partly because of the importance of trying to get something out of Ingram, but mostly because of what they were there to see.

A guard came to show them through to the prison's death row. The prison seemed quieter now than it had been, as if the whole place were holding its breath in expectation of what was to come. The guard took them through to a large viewing room, divided by a glass screen from the space in which the execution was to take place.

That execution chamber held a gurney waiting for Ingram to be strapped to it, along with a doctor who was presumably there to ensure that the lethal injection was set up correctly, and to certify death afterwards.

On their side of the glass, there were a few people there already, waiting in seats that made the whole space seem like some kind of particularly sober theater. Paige guessed that they were people with a connection to Lars Ingram's victims, or official observers there to make sure that everything proceeded smoothly. She saw a priest there among them, and a couple in late middle age who might have been the parents of one of Ingram's victims.

As Paige watched, two prison guards marched Ingram into the execution chamber. One was the young woman who had escorted them on their first visit, the other an older man Paige didn't know.

As he was marched in, Christopher stepped up to the glass, catching the attention of the guards. There was an intercom there; Paige guessed it was so that any last words by the prisoner or their loved ones could be heard. Christopher used it now.

"This is Agent Marriott with the FBI. We need one moment to speak with your prisoner."

"That's pretty irregular, Agent," the male guard said.

"Lives are at stake," Christopher replied.

Paige was already moving to the intercom. "Lars? I came, just like you asked. Now it's your turn to hold up your end of the deal."

Ingram looked over at her. He didn't look frightened, even now, but he did look resigned, as if he had come to terms with everything that was about to happen to him. The look he gave Paige wasn't friendly.

"So you came," he said. "Come to make sure that I'm dead?"

"You know why I'm here," Paige said. "I want the information you promised me on the man who has been copying you."

Lars laughed then. "You want something from me? Here? Now? What are you going to do to me if I don't tell you? Kill me?"

He laughed again, the only person in the room who seemed to find any of it funny. In that moment, Paige really could see the madness in him. This was a psychopath who didn't fear death, didn't seem to even care about what was about to happen to him.

"You don't have anything to offer me," he said, when he was done laughing. "I told you at the start of this that I wasn't going to give you information if you didn't have anything to give me in return."

"And we told you that we didn't have anything to offer," Christopher replied. "But you still seem to have promised Paige that you would give her information if she showed up here."

"Maybe I changed my mind," Ingram said. "I'll tell you what, get me a last-minute reprieve, and *then* I'll tell you something."

That was the biggest problem Paige and Christopher had: they didn't have anything that they could offer the serial killer. The one thing he wanted was something that wasn't in their power to grant. There was nothing they could give him now that could make his life easier, because that life was only going to last a few more minutes. There was no reprieve on the table, no chance of trading for information.

Paige tried to think of something else. They couldn't give Ingram anything, but maybe they could take something away. He wanted her here as a witness? Well, he was going to have to earn that.

"You went to a lot of trouble to get me here," she said. "But I came to get information. If you don't give me that information, I'll leave. You won't have the witness you want for your death."

"If you're going to make threats, you need to learn to do it better," Ingram said, apparently unperturbed.

"You think I won't walk away?" Paige asked. "You went to so much trouble to get me here, I don't think you'll let me do that."

Ingram shrugged, though. Apparently, he'd gotten all that he wanted just by getting her to come in the first place. "You'll stay. You won't be able to look away, once it starts. People are fascinated by death. They just don't have the guts to take the next step and actually kill someone." He turned to his guards. "We're done here."

They moved to march him to the gurney, and Paige knew that she was out of time. In just a few moments, Ingram's execution would begin, and there would be no further chance of getting anything out of him.

"Nikki Ashenko!" she called out in desperation.

She saw Ingram's head snap around at that. "What did you say?"

For the first time since she'd met him, Paige saw genuine shock on his features. He obviously hadn't ever imagined that she would find out about the young babysitter they'd found dead in the stream. She'd caught him off guard, and this was obviously the moment to try to push for more.

"Nikki Ashenko," Paige repeated. "We found her body earlier today. Forensic teams are there as we speak, and we know she couldn't have been killed by you. Your copycat has been operating almost from the start, hasn't he?"

Ingram didn't say anything yet, but Paige could see the troubled look on his face. She'd hit a nerve.

"Except that he's not just a copycat, is he?" Paige said. "He's more like a partner. Or maybe a competitor. My guess is that he's killed as many people as you."

The guards had paused again to let them keep talking, but Paige knew that she wouldn't have long. If this didn't work, then nothing would.

"You told me that we didn't know half of what you'd done. I bet there are more murders out there that are yours, but *these* ones? How many are his? How many of his kills are you dying for?"

She saw Ingram pause, obviously considering it, and he was silent for so long that the guards clearly assumed that he wasn't going to say anything. They took him to the gurney, strapping him down firmly and professionally.

"Braeburn!" Ingram shouted out suddenly, staring at Paige. It was just one word, and she had no idea how it related to anything else, but just the fact that Ingram had said it to her here and now told her that it was important.

"What? What does that mean?" Paige demanded, but Ingram was silent, making it clear that a single word was all they were going to get from him.

117

Christopher moved to Paige's side then. "He's told us everything he's going to. Frankly, I'm amazed you even got that out of him. We should go."

Paige shook her head, though. The deal she'd made with Ingram was that she would come to his execution, and he would give her information. Now that he'd given her something, she felt as if she couldn't just walk away. She couldn't renege on the deal, because that was the kind of thing that he might have done. More than that, it felt wrong not to stay, not to witness these last moments of a life, even one as wholly given over to evil acts as Ingram's was.

So, Paige sat there, staring through the glass screen as the guards finished strapping Ingram into place. She sat there as the priest stood up, reading Ingram the last rites via the intercom. It shouldn't have surprised Paige that a serial killer might be just as religious as anybody else, but somehow, it did.

The priest moved away then, and the doctor moved to insert a canula into Ingram's arm. He hooked it up to the machine that would deliver the lethal cocktail of drugs designed to kill him; Paige knew enough from her research to know that it would probably be pentobarbital first to sedate him, then pancuronium bromide to paralyze the respiratory system to prevent convulsions and also stop his breathing, and finally potassium chloride to stop the heart.

She watched while he was hooked up, and then the doctor moved to the side, waiting as if for the possibility of some last-minute reprieve. A clock in the corner clicked over onto the hour, and the doctor pushed a button to start the machine.

The stillness of it all was the strangest part. Paige saw Ingram tense against the straps that held him as the first of the drugs went into his system, but after that, he was still. His eyes slid shut and didn't open again. After a few minutes, the doctor moved forward to check him, and presumably pronounce him dead.

Just like that, a serial killer was gone. It was a much more peaceful end than any he'd given his victims. It seemed like too much and not enough, all at once, a deep well of emotions flowing up through Paige at the sight of him dead there. She didn't feel any grief for him in that moment, but she *did* feel it for his victims, and for all those his copycat had killed.

At least now, though, they had another clue that might help them catch that copycat before he struck again: Braeburn.

They just had to find out what it meant.

CHAPTER TWENTY THREE

Paige found her thoughts lingering on Lars Ingram's last moments as she and Christopher drove back towards the FBI headquarters. She knew that there should be a kind of grim satisfaction in knowing that the serial killer could never hurt anyone else, but her focus was on how little she'd managed to get from him.

One word. All that effort, all that time, all the horror of watching a man die in front of her, and Paige had only gotten a single word from Lars Ingram before he died. She didn't even know what it meant, if it meant anything at all.

It certainly didn't do anything to stop the copycat. He was still out there somewhere, and Paige was sure now that he'd killed far more people than the three that they knew about.

"I want to go back via the coroner's office," Christopher said. "Lamar is going to rush through his examination on the bones, and I want to be there when he does."

Paige nodded. That made sense to her. Any evidence they could get now might help them. Any scrap might be enough to point them in the right direction to stop the copycat killer before he struck again.

"Do you think there's any chance the killer might stop now?" Christopher asked.

Paige looked over to him. She hadn't really considered that possibility. "Why do you ask?"

"It looks like the killings were about the build up to the execution, right?" Christopher said.

Paige nodded. "That definitely looks like it was the spark for the last few killings. Certainly for them being so close together."

"So, now that it has happened, is it possible that the killer will decide that he has completed his 'tribute' to Ingram, or whatever it is he's doing, and he'll decide that there's no point in keeping going?"

Paige wished that it were that simple. "It's possible, but it doesn't seem likely. It's very rare that serial killers just stop. This one might take a break after the execution, but my guess is that he will feel the need again eventually, and act on it. Honestly, though, if he's been killing for three years now, my guess is that he will just keep going, trying to get in as many murders as possible without being caught."

That was a terrifying thought: that a serial killer might kill at a rate of one a day until they caught up to him. How many young women would lose their lives before he was finally apprehended?

"So not even a moment of breathing space," Christopher said. Perhaps he'd been hoping for a day or two in which to work the evidence without worrying about the lives that might be lost in the meantime.

Sadly, Paige had to disappoint him. "*Maybe* this killer will pause, but my guess is that he will keep going at his current rate now that he has realized that he can. It's like a drug fix for him. Now that he has ramped up, coming down from it and trying not to kill will feel almost physically painful."

Serial killers escalated and accelerated. Yes, some had gaps between their kills, but those were the ones who did so for reasons of ritual or because they tried to fight against the urge to kill for as long as possible. Now that this killer was killing rapidly, Paige doubted that he would go back to having gaps between his kills again. Either she and Christopher would catch him, or many more women were going to die. That was a terrifying thought, when they had so little to go on.

They arrived at the mortuary, heading through into a space that was cold enough to make Paige shiver, or maybe that was just down to the knowledge that there were bodies waiting for autopsies. The whole space had a very clean, very medical look to it, with even the waiting room looking like that of an expensive doctor's office.

Christopher nodded to the young woman at the reception desk. "Hey Janice. How are you?"

She was probably in her mid-twenties, with dark hair and heavy black makeup, plenty of tattoos showing on forearms left bare by the scrubs she wore.

"I'm fine thanks, Agent Marriott. You're here to see Dr. Neilson?"

Paige saw Christopher nod.

"Go straight through. He's expecting you."

They went through into an autopsy room where fleshless white bones were laid out on a table so that the coroner from the Nikki Ashenko murder scene could look at them. Several lamps shone down to provide almost painfully bright light for the examination, while a box held evidence bags with even the tiniest particulates labeled.

"Lamar," Christopher said. "How are things going with the autopsy for the body in the stream?"

"Slowly," Lamar replied. "How did you even find the body, Agent Marriott?"

"Paige here worked out what must have happened the night Nikki Ashenko went missing, and that allowed us to find her."

Lamar held up a warning finger.

"Assuming it *is* her," Christopher said, sounding as though the two of them had been through that conversation before.

"Better," Lamar said. "Although in this case, I have yet to find anything that isn't consistent with the hypothesis that this might be that young woman. Certainly, these are the bones of a woman in her early twenties, and given the location where you found them, it's enough for a tentative identification. I will have to wait for DNA results to provide something more substantial."

"Cause of death?" Christopher said.

Lamar gestured to the bones. "There is damage to the bones consistent with multiple deep knife wounds."

"Seven?" Paige asked.

"At least four," Lamar said, "but it is possible that other wounds were present without damage to the bones."

So there was nothing there to suggest that this *wasn't* Nikki Ashenko. If there had been a dozen stab wounds, that would have been a problem, but as it was, Paige's theory that this was the copycat still held.

"What physical evidence were you able to recover from the body?" Christopher asked.

"After three years in a stream?" Lamar said. "Almost nothing. DNA and prints have been washed away. There's no flesh left, so there won't be any evidence to recover from that. Frankly, we don't even have a full skeleton yet. At least some of the smaller bones are still missing. My guess is that they were carried further downstream."

Which meant that they weren't going to get anything that was going to lead them to the door of the killer.

"Is there anything you *can* give us?" Christopher asked.

"Given time, I should be able to provide the dimensions of the blade used, so that if you recover one, I'll be able to match it to the one employed."

"Have you done that with the other cases?" Paige asked.

"The ones that I've seen. There should be similar profiles in the reports for any other cases," Lamar said.

Meaning that they potentially had a way to work out which murders had been committed by which killers.

"Were all of the most recent murders committed using the same knife?" Paige asked.

"Yes, I believe so."

Meaning that the copycat killer kept the same weapon for each murder. That might also prove to be useful.

At the same time, though, it didn't seem as though it was enough. It wasn't as if knives were registered like handguns. There was no way to trace a knife back to the killer even if they could identify it precisely. The best they could do was to use the evidence to link the killer to the crime once they caught him.

They still had to do that, and it seemed as if the only way they had to go about it was to follow the clue that Lars Ingram had given them.

"Thank you for your time," Christopher said. "Can you call me directly if you find any evidence that might lead us back to the killer?"

"Of course," Lamar said.

The two of them headed back out to the car, and there, Paige got her laptop out.

"Do you want to head back to the office?" Christopher asked.

"I want to try to find out what Ingram meant when he said Braeburn," Paige replied. "It has to mean something."

Christopher gave her a serious look. "It's possible that it doesn't. Ingram was a psychopath. This could be just another way to mess with us."

Paige knew that was a possibility, but she also didn't believe it, not entirely.

"You saw how he was caught off guard," Paige said. "I think that he *kept* it to one word to mess with us, but I think the word itself means something. The question is what."

"All right, start checking, see if you can find anything that might be relevant," Christopher said. "Check police records, the DMV, everything you can."

Paige checked the records, and the problem wasn't an absence of hits, but an overabundance of them. Even though the name wasn't that common, it was still common enough to bring in hits from around the country, with no way of telling which might be relevant or not.

Paige needed to try a different approach. She started to look back into Lars Ingram's history instead. There was a lot there, but at least she knew that any mention was going to be relevant. She looked back through the case files, looking for any mention of the word Braeburn.

The murder files didn't have any mention of the word, but Paige kept going as Christopher drove back towards the office, looking through news reports, trying to find any kind of mention.

When she found it, it wasn't the name of a person, but of a company: Braeburn contracting services. It was there, buried in the transcript of a podcast devoted to Lars Ingram's crimes, the kind of thing that wasn't trying to do the kind of research Paige had been doing, but instead was mostly trying to get the maximum entertainment value from the viciousness of the crimes.

Paige looked into the business further, and now that she had a starting point, she was able to find more, able to narrow down the mess of references to Braeburn and find the ones that mattered. She found the company that Lars Ingram had worked for, then found the records to establish exactly who had been involved with it.

Just one other man, named Cal Sanders.

The fact that Ingram had named the company rather than just giving Paige his name worried her a little, but maybe that was just his way of making her work harder, forcing her to jump through more hoops even after his death.

Whatever the reason, Paige couldn't afford to ignore Cal Sanders.

Paige ran that name next, and quickly found that he had a record. A *long* record. He'd been in and out of prison multiple times and was no stranger at all to violence. Paige pulled up his files, and those files troubled her even more, because there were psych assessments there relating to one of his cases. Those contained details of the small crimes he'd committed as a child, the time he'd been caught hurting a neighbor's dog, a kid who'd been hurt when no one could prove it wasn't an accident.

It was the kind of file that pointed to a psychopath, and maybe to more.

Paige forced herself not to get too excited. She didn't want to send her and Christopher running off after another lead only for it to fall apart. She checked Sanders's prison record, wanting to make sure that he wasn't inside at the time of any of the murders, but it seemed that he'd been out for at least the last three years.

Had he come out of prison, met up with his old friend Lars Ingram, and decided to join in with the darkest side of the man's life?

"I think we have something," Paige said, finally satisfied. "A man who used to work with Lars Ingram at Braeburn Contracting Services. He has a violent history, and he was out of prison at the time of the murders."

"Do you have an address for him?" Christopher asked.

Paige nodded. "He lives in D.C., out in the suburbs."

Meaning that he was still in the area, still there to commit the murders.

"Then we need to go talk to this guy right away."

CHAPTER TWENTY FOUR

Paige watched Cal Sanders's home, trying to establish if he was there before she and Christopher moved in. It was one of the things they'd taught her in training: that the observation phase of a raid was almost as important as actually making the arrest. This was the phase where they could establish a precise location for a suspect, work out if they were walking into any kind of danger, and plan so that their suspect had no chance of getting away.

Yet there was only so long they could wait and watch. It was getting late. If the killer was going to strike again today, then this might be their last chance to stop him.

For now, doing that meant watching a quiet suburban home that had been extensively renovated so that it wasn't quite the square, boxy construction of the rest of the street, but instead had been extended well into the yard, suggesting that Cal Sanders had brought his contracting skills to bear on his own home.

"I think you should wait in the car while I make the arrest," Christopher said, holding the warrant that they'd been able to get based on what Lars Ingram had given them. "I told Agent Podovski that I wouldn't lead you into danger, and we have no idea what might be in there."

"That's why I *should* be there," Paige argued. She had no wish to be left behind now, even if it was meant to be for her own safety. She wanted to be a part of this. "You shouldn't go up against a potential serial killer alone. You need someone to back you up."

"You haven't finished your training yet, Paige," Christopher pointed out.

"I faced up to Adam Riker alone."

He'd trusted her to do that, but was trying to protect her now?

"All right," Christopher said. "But you stay close to me. Remember that you're not armed, so don't start trying to tackle a man who likes to stab his victims."

Paige wasn't planning to do that, but she also wasn't going to just hang back and leave all of this to Christopher. She could be an extra set of eyes to try to make sure that Cal Sanders didn't ambush them, at least.

It also meant that she was able to spot a flicker of movement there in one of the upstairs windows.

"He's in there," Paige said. "The only question now is how we do this."

"A guy who's been in and out of prison will spot me as law enforcement before I make it to the door if I just go up to the front," Christopher said. "That might give him time to run."

"So you want to go around the back?" Paige asked.

Christopher shook his head. "Our best chance of grabbing Sanders is at his door. We aren't in an unfamiliar environment that way, where he might be able to get to a weapon or escape."

Paige thought she understood then. "You want me to distract him?"

Christopher nodded. "If you're serious about wanting to help with this. I'll come in from the side, out of sight of the windows. When I do, I want you to walk up to the door, ring the bell, and get him to answer."

Paige knew that there were risks in that. If they didn't time it right, or if Sanders became suspicious, then she could find herself facing off against a serial killer alone for however many seconds it took Christopher to get there.

Yet she also knew that it was the safest way for them to do this, minimizing the chance that Sanders would get away to kill more women or turn this into a running battle. For that, Paige was prepared to take the risk.

"All right," Paige said. "Let's do this."

She got out of the car, moving slowly towards the door of the house, giving Christopher time to hurry around to the side, approaching Cal Sanders 's property via his neighbor's yard. Paige watched him move along the side of a garage, and at the same time, she kept moving forward, almost up to the door now.

Her heart was in her mouth as she rang the bell. This had been easy to agree to in the car, but now that she was actually doing it, Paige could feel a thread of fear running through her. Even so, she forced herself to smile.

Paige heard movement from inside, and a few moments later, the door opened, revealing a man in his late thirties, badly shaven and heavily muscled, wearing slacks and a dark sweater. Exactly the kind of thing that might make him less memorable when he was approaching a target.

"Yeah?" he said.

"Cal Sanders?" Paige said, in the brightest, friendliest tone she could manage.

"Who wants to know?"

Christopher answered that one, stepping out into the open with his weapon already raised. "FBI. Don't move. You're under arrest."

To Paige's surprise, he didn't try to run then, didn't try to slam the door in their faces. He didn't try to fight, although she guessed that the gun pointed at him might have plenty to do with that.

Paige expected a lot of things, but she *didn't* expect a resigned sigh from Sanders.

"I've been expecting you."

*

They took him back to the FBI headquarters and put him in an interrogation room, moving in to sit opposite him under the unblinking gaze of a camera. To Paige, he looked like he was projecting an attempt to appear calm and in control, but she could see the nerves underneath it, too. This was a man who had been around the justice system too many times to believe that any of this was good for him.

"So, Cal," Christopher said. "When I arrested you, you said that you'd been expecting us. Do you want to tell us what you meant by that?"

"I'm not saying anything until my lawyer gets here," Sanders retorted.

"So it doesn't have anything to do with the fact that you knew your killing spree would lead to you getting caught eventually?" Christopher tried. "Was that it, Cal? You knew that Ingram would give you up, so you wanted to kill as many women as you could before we caught up to you?"

Sanders was silent, then, simply shaking his head to make it clear that he wasn't going to say anything else. When Christopher gestured to the door, Paige went with him. The two of them could always look into the room via a screen set up just outside.

"Do you think that we'll be able to get him to talk?" Christopher asked.

Obviously, he had more experience with interrogations than Paige did, but she guessed that he wanted her opinion because of her

127

psychological expertise. It was nice to know that he respected that, but even so, Paige wasn't sure quite what to tell him then.

"It will depend on why he's done this," she said. "If what you said in there is true, and this does prove to be a last spree, knowing that he'll be caught, then maybe he'll want to claim credit for it."

"But he might not?" Christopher asked.

"He might still think that he can get away with it by staying silent," Paige pointed out. "We don't have much in the way of direct physical evidence, and while the dying words of a serial killer might have been enough for a warrant, I doubt they'll convince a jury."

"Forensic teams are already searching his house," Christopher said. "Anything that links to any of the dead women, and we'll have him."

Paige could see that he was itching to get back in there and put pressure on Sanders, but for now, all the two of them could do was wait there, watching him while they waited for the lawyer to show up.

"He looks more nervous than he's letting on," Paige said. He certainly didn't seem to share Ingram's lack of fear. Did that mean that he didn't have that almost pure, uncompromising psychopathy that Ingram had possessed? Did that mean that he might actually respond to an appeal based on the humanity of his victims, or simply to the fear of what might happen next if he didn't talk?

Paige was still contemplating it when a prim woman in her forties approached the interrogation room, wearing an expensively cut pantsuit and carrying a briefcase. She had dark hair, high cheekbones, and piercing dark eyes that currently held deep disapproval.

"Are *you* the agents who decided to arrest my client based on nothing more than the word of a serial killer?" she demanded.

"I'm Agent Marriott," Christopher said. "This is my consultant, Paige King."

"And I am Audrey Lowerstoft, of Marlin and Lowerstoft. You will release my client at once."

"Not when he's our lead suspect in multiple murder cases," Christopher shot back, "and *certainly* not when we haven't questioned him yet."

"You have nothing on him," Ms. Lowerstoft said.

Christopher didn't look impressed. "We have a long history of criminal behavior, some of it violent. We have his personal history with Lars Ingram, which might have allowed him to learn Ingram's methods. And, as you said, we *do* have the word of a serial killer. Ingram's dying confession of who his partner was."

"More like his dying act of revenge," Ms. Lowerstoft said. She held out a piece of paper. When Christopher didn't take it, Paige did, reading through it.

"It's an immunity agreement," Paige said. "Sanders was let off assault and possession of an illegal firearm charges in return for information leading to Ingram's arrest."

Christopher looked doubtful at that. "Ingram was caught because DNA linked him to one of his crimes."

"Once he was caught, that helped to convict him," Ms. Lowerstoft replied. "But my client's information was what got them to that point. This is a petty act of revenge on Lars Ingram's part."

Was this possible? Was it really possible that Lars Ingram had played her, even as he was about to die?

The reality of that hit Paige all at once. Ingram had played her, the way Adam Riker had played her before, sending her down a blind alley, lying because he could. The sheer similarity of it meant that Paige believed it, *knew* that it was true, even as she hated it.

Paige cursed to herself at having been taken in by Ingram, at having been played by him again. From the start of this, he'd wanted to waste her time, and had shown no interest in catching the real killer, yet she'd been willing to believe that a psychopath might tell the truth just as he was about to die?

Christopher still looked determined, though. "I still want to question Sanders. He might have given Ingram up, but that could just have been to get rid of his competition as a killer."

"Do you really believe that?" Ms. Lowerstoft asked.

"I think that we'll know a lot more once we've questioned your client," Christopher said.

The three of them went through into the interrogation room, where Ms. Lowerstoft took a seat beside Cal Sanders. Not too close, Paige noticed, as if this were a distasteful duty she had to perform. She obviously didn't think much of her client, but then, she didn't have to *like* Sanders to defend him.

"Where were you the last three nights?" Christopher asked, once they were all settled.

Sanders shrugged. "At home."

"Can anyone confirm that?"

That got another shrug. "I live alone."

129

Meaning that he had no real alibi. Paige could see Christopher's excitement at that. He really thought that they had their man, that Sanders had given up Ingram to let him keep killing with impunity.

Paige wasn't sure if she believed that, though, for one simple reason: the killings had stopped when Ingram was caught. The copycat had paused in his grim work in a way that someone effectively trying to take over from Ingram wouldn't have.

More than that, the more she thought about Ingram, the more Paige realized that him trying to take revenge fit his personality more than him helping to stop a killer, even as he was about to be executed.

"What about the 19th of April three years ago?" Christopher asked.

"How am I meant to remember something like that?" Sanders snapped back.

"What happened on that date?" Ms. Lowerstoft asked.

Christopher fixed Sanders with a baleful look. "That's when your client murdered a young woman called Nikki Ashenko, isn't it, Sanders?"

Sanders shook his head. "I didn't have anything to do with any of this. I-"

"I would like an opportunity to consult with my client before there are any further questions," Ms. Lowerstoft said.

Christopher didn't look happy about it, but he stood, and Paige went with him. Suspects had the right to consult their lawyers. When they got outside, Paige could see Christopher buzzing with the need to get back in there and get Sanders to confess. It only made the next thing she had to say that much harder.

"I don't think Cal Sanders did this, Christopher."

CHAPTER TWENTY FIVE

Paige had fully expected the surprise that spread across Christopher's face as she said the words.

"What do you mean, you don't think he did it?" Christopher said. He sounded like he couldn't quite believe that she'd said it, and then led Paige a few paces away from the interrogation room, over to a space where a watercooler stood. Maybe to anyone looking on, this would have looked like just another watercooler conversation about a case at the FBI, but with the animation on Christopher's face, Paige doubted it.

"I don't think he did it," Paige repeated. "I think his lawyer is right: this is just another way for Lars Ingram to mess with us."

Christopher was already shaking his head as Paige said it, though. "Paige, she's *paid* to be convincing. It's literally her job to come up with good arguments and cast doubt on anything we think is true."

"But in this case, I think she has a point," Paige said. "Ingram just happened to give us the name of the guy who gave *him* up to the authorities? It's the easiest way for him to get revenge. If Sanders ends up on death row, it will be everything Ingram could hope for."

"And how did he *know* enough to give Ingram up?" Christopher asked. "How did Cal Sanders know that Lars Ingram was a serial killer when he'd fooled the rest of the world? Unless Sanders was working with him?"

That was the other part of this, though.

"The cases don't read like a pair working together," Paige pointed out. For her, that was another strike against Sanders being guilty. "These were cases by two separate individuals, not one person working with another to commit the crimes. If the two knew each other that well, why didn't they commit the murders side by side?"

Christopher didn't look convinced by Paige's argument, though.

"Maybe they did, a couple of times. Then maybe the Nikki Ashenko murder was Sanders branching out. Maybe the two fell out, and that's why he gave Ingram up."

"And why didn't Ingram give Sanders up in return back then?" Paige asked. To her, it didn't add up. There was no reason for Ingram to keep Sanders's identity a secret for years, only to then hand it to her at the point of his death.

She could see the frustration on Christopher's face.

"Paige, this is the first time in this case we've had a solid suspect, and it's because of work *you* did. Good work. You want to throw that away now based on what? A feeling that this isn't the right guy?"

"It's more than a feeling," Paige said. "The information that he was the informant changes everything."

"Not for me," Christopher said.

"Well, maybe you're just being stubborn." As soon as Paige said it, she knew that it was the wrong thing to say.

"And maybe you're not sticking with a theory long enough, Paige. This isn't academia, where you get to jump from one hypothesis to the next and nobody cares."

"Is that what you think I did with my time in my PhD?" Paige snapped. She knew that it was just the pressure of the case getting to her, but still, she found that she was annoyed with Christopher belittling what she'd achieved like that.

"I think that if you got things wrong there, nobody died," Christopher said. "Whereas now, if we let Cal Sanders back on the street and another woman dies tonight, that's on us."

"And if he's not the killer?" Paige said. "What then? We sit here questioning him while the real killer is out there, free to do as he pleases?"

"I'm the agent running this case," Christopher said. "I'm the one who has to decide. You're still just a trainee. There won't be any comeback on you if this goes wrong."

"Was I *just* a trainee when I helped to catch Adam Riker?" Paige shot back. This was the closest thing the two of them had ever had to an argument.

"No, you were a civilian. Now that you're trying to become an FBI agent, you're going to have to learn to follow through on the leads, all the way to the end."

Paige couldn't contain her frustration at that. "Maybe this would be easier for you if I weren't here."

"If you're not going to help get answers out of Sanders, then maybe. I'm going to take the rest of this interrogation alone."

He headed back into the interrogation room, leaving Paige behind.

A part of her knew that she ought to follow, ought to play her part in the interrogation, but more of her still believed that they had the wrong man, and that Christopher was being completely unreasonable about it.

Paige knew why: if this wasn't their guy, then they had no evidence to lead them to someone else. They had to accept that the killer was still out there, and that there was no immediate way to stop him from killing more women. Of course, she could also see why Christopher thought that Sanders was a good suspect. It was just that he didn't fit, not here, not now.

Paige realized then that she didn't fit, either. Christopher had called her in on this case for advice, but now he wasn't listening to that advice. So, what was the point of being there at all? She needed to get out of there.

The moment Paige had that thought, she knew that it was absolutely true. She couldn't be there in the FBI headquarters right then. She couldn't just stand out there while Christopher took another run at Sanders.

She started walking, grabbing her laptop from Christopher's office and heading down to the street. Paige caught a cab there, not quite knowing what to do next.

"Where to?" the driver asked.

Paige was about to give the address for her apartment, when she realized that if she went there feeling like this, she would just sit there, still not knowing what to do, not quite achieving anything.

She could go back to the academy, but what would it look like if she went there now? It would seem as though she'd been thrown off the case. It would seem as if she wasn't up to the life of being an FBI agent.

Maybe she wasn't. So far, Paige hadn't been close to good enough at the physical aspects of the training, and if Christopher didn't trust her judgement either, what did that say about her prospects as an agent? Nothing good.

"Where to, lady?" the driver asked again.

Paige knew then where she needed to go: to the place where she'd always gone when she'd been having trouble with her thesis. To the friend and mentor that she knew she could rely on.

She needed to go see Professor Thornton.

*

133

The Thorntons' place was large and timber framed, old and well cared for, and even pulling up there felt as though it let Paige relax a little. She'd been there so many times, and always received a warm welcome. For a long time, when she and her mother hadn't really been talking, the Thorntons had been like a family Paige had chosen.

Haley Thornton met her at the door, in her fifties, round faced and pleasantly plump, with a cheerful smile. She had spiked blonde hair and a large collection of piercings through both ears.

"Paige!" she said, stepping forward to give Paige a hug. That was simply the kind of welcome Paige got here. "We weren't expecting you today. We thought you'd be training over at the academy. Wait, your face… what's wrong?"

Paige knew better than to try to hide her unhappiness right then. "I was helping Agent Marriott with another case and things… they're wrong. I don't know what to do next."

Haley held her out at arm's length. "It sounds as if you need to talk to Francis. Come in, he's in his study. You know the way by now. I'll bring coffee through."

Paige *did* know the way. She'd been to this house, and this study, more times than she could count. Paige went to it now, and although the door was open, she still knocked.

Professor Thornton was in his fifties, tall where his wife was short, with a short dark beard with more gray in it than he probably liked. He was sitting in a brown leather office chair. He was dressed in khaki slacks and a cream shirt, while glasses rested on his nose. The study around him seemed to fit like a glove, every inch of the walls given over to shelves holding a mixture of books, ornaments, and pictures. Paige was surprised but pleased to see a picture from her own graduation there among it all.

"Paige, it's good to see you," he said with a smile as he saw her. He gestured to a hardbacked chair set against the wall. "Please, come in, take a seat. I wasn't expecting to see you today."

"No… I… I'm sorry, I don't know what to do next," Paige said, as she took the seat.

"Are things not going well with your training?" Prof. Thornton said. "Or is it something else? Your mother, perhaps?"

"No, everything's fine with mom," Paige replied. "Have you… have you seen the murders that have been in the news the last few days?"

"It's hard to avoid them," Prof. Thornton said. He looked at Paige with a sudden note of concern. "Wait, are you involved with the investigation somehow? But you haven't completed your training yet."

"Agent Marriott asked me for my help," Paige said. "Only now... I think we have the wrong suspect, and I can't convince him."

"Then maybe you need more evidence."

That seemed easy to say, harder to put into practice.

"Where am I going to get more evidence?" Paige said. "Christopher's right, I'm not an agent. I can't just go out and start questioning witnesses or demanding that forensics give me whatever they have."

"No," Prof. Thornton said. "But that's not why you're on this case, is it, Paige?"

"What do you mean?" Paige asked.

"If you're helping with a case, it's because Agent Marriott believes that you can provide an insight into the killer, yes?"

"Well... yes," Paige admitted.

"And now you're stuck because you don't know who to look at next."

Paige nodded. She didn't know what to do next.

"Then you're focusing on the wrong thing," Prof. Thornton said.

Paige frowned at that.

"You're a psychologist, Paige. Don't focus on the who, focus on the why. What does this man want that has him killing so many women right now? What is so important to him that he's doing it here, like this, now?"

As he said that, Paige realized that the professor had a point. She'd been running around with Christopher, trying to conduct what was essentially a conventional investigation. She'd gotten so caught up in the need to find standard evidence, in alibis and opportunities, that she'd forgotten just how much it might be possible to find just by working on the parts of the case that *were* in her wheelhouse.

She needed to work out what the killer was trying to accomplish with this spree. If she could understand that, maybe she might be able to work out where he would strike next.

CHAPTER TWENTY SIX

Paige was anxious as she returned to her apartment, but also driven. She wasn't going there to sit on the couch and wallow in despair, the way she might have before talking to Professor Thornton.

The killer was still out there, so she only had a short amount of time. She needed somewhere that she could work.

Until she had this figured out, Paige suspected that the FBI offices were out. She didn't want to go back there only to find Christopher still trying to pressure Cal Sanders to confess. She wouldn't be free there to work on the things that she wanted. Either she would have to help with trying to find proof that Sanders was a murderer when she didn't believe that he was, or she was going to face the potential of another argument with Christopher about why she wasn't helping.

Maybe the news of the first argument had already gotten around. Maybe it was working its way back to her superiors at the academy even as Paige thought about it. It was possible that at any moment, she might receive a call telling her that she had to return, if only so that they could tell her formally that she would never be an FBI agent.

Paige just hoped that she could come up with something before that point.

Her apartment felt strange as she settled down in it with her laptop. She hadn't been there in weeks now, since she started at the academy, so everything felt strangely still and untouched there, more of a repository of memories than a place currently lived in. This had been where Paige had finished her thesis, where she'd made the decision to join the FBI, where she'd decided the whole course of her life to come.

Now, it was where she needed to learn more about a killer.

Paige didn't have the board with her timeline on it; that was back in Christopher's office in the FBI building. Still, she had enough notes and files on her computer to recreate it now, sticking a large piece of paper to her refrigerator with fridge magnets and drawing on it with a set of multi-colored markers she found half buried in a kitchen drawer.

Paige wrote the three most recent murders in blue, for cases that were definitely the work of the copycat killer. She added in Nikki

Ashenko's death in the same color. The other murder on the same day went in red, to show that it was definitely Lars Ingram's work.

Those were the only certainties, so the other murders went on there in yellow, for the moment, ready to be underlined in one color or the other as Paige made progress.

Her next avenue of investigation was to go through what she could find of the case against Lars Ingram. The murder he'd been tied to with DNA seemed as though it could be confidently underlined in red.

There were some where he appeared to have admitted to them after his conviction. That caught Paige's interest. Why those, and not others? She marked the ones he'd admitted to in red, with the others.

Where did that leave her? Not far enough along, not yet. Paige found herself remembering Ingram's words to her: "You don't know half of what I've done." Assuming as before that he meant that he'd committed far more murders than people thought, she added in the missing persons cases that she and Christopher had managed to identify before as possibly linked to the case.

Ok, so she had a timeline. Now what?

This was the point where Paige had gotten distracted by the Nikki Ashenko murder before. Now, though, she stared at the timeline, hoping that it would unlock its secrets. She kept staring at it, trying to think of all the ways that she might be able to differentiate between cases that were Lars Ingram's work and those that were the work of the other killer; it seemed almost wrong to call him just a copycat by now. He was a colleague, an equal. A... rival?

That thought made Paige take another look at the timeline. Did it do anything to help her find patterns there in the data she had? Finding that kind of pattern was something she was supposedly good at, thanks to her PhD. So where were the patterns here?

Paige kept looking, walked away, and came back to stare at the timeline once again. One thing stood out to her: There was a point, shortly before the Nikki Ashenko murder, when the volume of potential kills suddenly went up. In theory, that kind of escalation could happen with one killer, but since Paige already knew that there were two, it seemed reasonable to her to assume that it might have been then that the second killer began his own, parallel spree.

That still didn't solve the problem of attributing kills to either Ingram or the copycat, except that it gave all the kills before that point definitively to Ingram. Paige underlined them in red, although honestly, it only gave her three more cases that were absolutely Ingram's.

What about the rest? How was she meant to go about dividing those, when there seemed to be no real pattern to the data? When the kills seemed not to take place at regular intervals, but in lumps and clusters, with a couple of murders maybe happening close together and then a gap?

Paige tried looking for a pattern in the data by trying to draw waveforms over the timeline, trying to see if each killer had his own rhythm, and if the presence of the other's work was only obscuring that. There was nothing as regular as that, though.

Paige went and sat down on the couch. It was impossible not to feel a little dejected. She wasn't solving this the way she'd hoped. She'd thought that the patterns would be there in the data, obvious to see. She'd thought that it would make it easy to come to a conclusion.

What did the copycat want?

That was the problem: there could be plenty of different things he might want. He might want to continue what he saw as Ingram's glorious work. He might want to just keep killing as many people as possible before he was caught. He might want to transition to another method of killing now that the figure he was copying was dead. He might be doing this for the fame, for a sense of power, for the challenge, or simply because some voice in his head told him that he had to.

It was even possible, although Paige doubted it, that he might see his work as complete and just stop, at least for now.

When her takeout order came, Paige found that she wasn't hungry after all. She couldn't settle, and went downstairs to walk around the block, hoping that the physical activity would make it easier to think. Some of her best ideas for her thesis had come while walking in one of the local parks, or sitting on a bench, trying to think of anything else other than work.

Paige left her phone behind as she walked. She suspected that, at some point, Christopher would come out of his interrogation of Cal Sanders for long enough to see that she was gone, and at that point, he would start to message her to try to get her to come back.

Or maybe he wouldn't, and that would be worse.

Paige walked, and as she walked, she looked around herself at the streets of D.C. The local park wasn't far now, just across the next street. Paige could feel herself relaxing a little as she walked, but that relaxation wasn't absolute. There was still a part of her that was working on the case, trying to understand the copycat killer better, trying to find a way into his personality and motivation that might allow her to predict what he was going to do next. He was out there somewhere, might be stalking his next victim even now.

She was still thinking about it when her eyes fell on a couple of public tennis courts set in the park, there for anyone who wanted to play for fun or exercise. Currently a couple of kids in their teens were running back and forth, hitting the ball to one another, sustaining a long rally until finally the ball thudded into the chain link fence around the court and one of them whooped in triumph.

Paige almost echoed the sound as she saw the win, because in that moment, she thought that she understood. She turned and ran back towards her home, darting back across the street, oblivious to a car whose horn blared as it only barely missed her. She had to get back before the shape of this idea fled from her. She had to see the timeline again to be sure.

Paige ran up the stairs to her apartment, kind of grateful now for the improved fitness that the FBI's training program had started to give her. She reached the door to her apartment, let herself in, and ran over to her refrigerator.

The timeline was still there, but now, Paige could see the pattern in it, the one that she'd been missing. It wasn't about any kind of regular interval between kills but was instead all about the grouping of kills.

In every case after the Nikki Ashenko murder, one kill was closely followed by a second, usually just a few days after it. There were a couple of spots where that led to a third and fourth kill, too, as if the two had been going back and forth, bouncing murders between them like some deadly game of tennis.

It was call and response. One, Paige guessed Lars Ingram, would kill, and then the other would manage a kill of his own. Paige looked at the files for the murders, and she saw something else, too: the second murders were always at least as difficult as the first. Where Ingram took an easy kill in an almost empty house, so did the second killer. Yet on an occasion where Ingram had killed an au pair while her entire host family was home, the next kill had been a nurse working overnight in a clinic, where there was very little chance of controlling the surrounding environment.

This killer didn't just want to copy Ingram; he wanted to *beat* him.

Paige felt as though she could start to divide up the board now, with the first of any pair going to Ingram, the second to the copycat. It meant that, in the period when both had been active, they'd killed the same number of people, but Ingram had always had that nagging head start of those three original kills.

So in the days leading up to Ingram's execution, the killer had deliberately made three kills of his own, wanting to level the tally before his rival, his competitor, died.

That wouldn't be enough, though, would it? Being level with Ingram wasn't going to satisfy this killer. If Paige understood what was happening, then he wasn't going to settle for just tying this game with Ingram. He was going to want to *win* it, maybe to take over as the undisputed champion of their deadly, sick game. He was going to want to make one more kill.

It had to be today, didn't it? That part seemed almost obvious now that Paige thought about it. The one-upping of Ingram's kills said to her that this killer cared about the way things were done, as well as the numbers. He wouldn't let the day of Ingram's death go unmarked.

It wouldn't just be any kill, either. For the one that let him win, the killer wouldn't want some run of the mill, easy victory. He would want something that represented a challenge, something that was meaningful. Now, Paige just had to work out what, and she needed to work it out now. With the killer still out there, there was no time left.

CHAPTER TWENTY SEVEN

He was sharpening his knife, the slow scrape of the steel across the whetstone both rhythmical and soothing. He'd used it so much in the last few days that he wanted to be sure that it still held its edge.

There was still work to do with it.

That was why he ground the edge carefully, making sure to keep an accurate angle throughout. Precision was important, in this as in the art of killing.

And it *was* an art. Lars Ingram had shown him that.

Not that they'd ever met, or even spoken. There had been a temptation to try, but honestly, what would he have said? "You're my hero" would have sounded far too fanboyish, and in any case, he wasn't sure that it was true. Ingram was an inspiration, even a template, but a hero?

He continued to sharpen the blade, moving to a finer grit of whetstone, while he contemplated the problem. He did the sharpening in the kitchen of his home, so that in the unlikely event that anyone saw, they would think that he was thinking of cutting nothing more than a good steak.

Had Lars Ingram ever been his hero? Even at the start of all this, it had felt more like he was the one setting a problem to be solved, rather than an awe-inspiring figure. Yes, there was the sense that Ingram was probably the only other person out there who might understand what it was like to feel this way, but that didn't mean that there was any kind of relationship there.

That was one reason he'd never called Ingram in prison. The other was that he'd always known the time would come when he would start killing again. It would have been foolish to leave any record that might lead back to him. He had no doubt that, following his kills, the FBI would have been through every scrap of paper sent to Ingram, checked the identity of every caller he'd ever had.

He wasn't sure what to make of the FBI. He'd seen the agent in charge of the case on the news, of course: Agent Christopher Marriott, of the BAU. There was the woman with him, as well, the one from all the news coverage around the Adam Riker case: Paige King.

141

On the one hand, he relished the presence of two people with an obvious record of tracking killers. It meant that there was an edge to this game, even in the absence of Lars Ingram. On the other, they hardly seemed like worthy opponents. They weren't even truly playing the game, since they weren't racking up kills of their own. They were simply trying to spoil it for him.

But then, maybe that was just a sign that the nature of the game was shifting. Perhaps in the future, it would no longer be him against Ingram, but him against the forces of the FBI.

He switched from the fine whetstone to a barber's strop as he considered that, working the blade quickly along it. This knife had killed so many people by now. He'd kept it with him ever since that first kill. Ever since the night Nikki Ashenko had died screaming and begging in a stream.

He had refined his technique considerably since then.

He needed it to be perfect today. From tomorrow, the game might be changed, but today, there was still the matter of getting that one kill better than Ingram had. It had to be today. The last day of Ingram's life. It was significant. It mattered. Taking a kill tomorrow wouldn't just be less satisfying. It would be… cheating.

Satisfied with the sharpness of the knife now, he tested it against the hairs of his left arm. It was sharp enough to shave them. More than sharp enough to kill cleanly, perfectly, tonight.

That would be his victory when it came to Ingram, but it would be more than that. He'd saved up these last few kills deliberately. He could have killed four people at any point after Ingram had found himself imprisoned, but he'd wanted it to be on these last few days leading up to Ingram's death specifically. It was more significant that way, but it also did a better job of attracting attention.

He *wanted* that attention. He'd been in Ingram's shadow for too long.

Today would change that. The kills so far had gotten the attention of both the press and the FBI, but his next would secure his place as a legend in his own right. It was a more audacious kill than anything Ingram had taken on. He'd killed weak people, young women with no hope of fighting back. Even when Nikki Ashenko had tried to fight in *his* first kill, it hadn't even come close to making a difference.

This target had the potential to fight back. She was trained, potentially dangerous. She'd handled killers before, but also cared for them, spoken with them, spent time with them. She was as much a caretaker to them as the young women he'd killed before had been to old women and children.

She met all criteria that Lars Ingram's work had set in place, and now, she had enough of a link to him for this to be special. He'd even watched her up close, sitting in the small crowd at the execution, watching as she watched Lars Ingram die.

Yes, he decided as he put the knife away carefully, *this* kill would be perfect.

CHAPTER TWENTY EIGHT

Paige knew what the killer wanted, but she still had to work out where and when he was going to strike. In theory, he could kill anyone, anywhere, but Paige had to believe that it wouldn't be as random as that.

This was the day of Lars Ingram's death, and the killer's chance to "win" the competition between the two of them. Would he really kill someone random for that moment? No, Paige was sure that the moment meant too much to the killer for that.

He would want this to be meaningful, to be special to him. The only question was how he was going to make it special. What was the component for him that was going to make this meaningful?

Paige started slightly as she realized that it was all about the connection to Ingram. The killer would want to find a way to simultaneously mark Ingram's death and declare that he had surpassed him. He would want something that was a suitably impressive challenge, too. Paige couldn't imagine him wanting to kill just anyone for this.

Paige started to look through everything she had on Ingram, trying to find someone who would fit that description. Perhaps someone Ingram had always wanted to kill but had never been able to get to? No, there was no record of him having spoken about that, and unless he had, how would the killer know who to go after?

No, it had to be something else, *someone* else. Was there anyone from Ingram's past who might make a suitable target? Paige couldn't see anybody obvious. There was no one who worked as a caretaker in his past other than his victims, as far as Paige could see.

The truth was that there wasn't a lot for her to go on. There was a lot of writing out there about Ingram, and Paige found a little speculation about who his next victims might have been, but the writers didn't provide any real evidence why he might have picked one victim over another. It just seemed to be a collection of people the authors wanted to see dead.

It didn't help. The problem was how little information Paige had. If she'd only gotten more out of Ingram when she'd gone to the prison to talk to him, she might have an answer now, but instead, she'd gotten nothing real before he called for the guards to take him back to his cell.

The guards.

Paige found herself thinking of the young female prison guard who had brought him to the interview room that first time, who had brought him to his execution. What had her name been? Nadia?

Wasn't guarding Ingram at the moment of his death the ultimate in care? Wasn't it exactly the kind of connection that a killer might want for this last, meaningful kill? He probably wouldn't know who the guards had been at Ingram's execution but would have been easy for him to find out that this guard had worked on death row, that she'd cared for Ingram from day to day while he was waiting for his death.

She would have meaning to Ingram's life, she would probably prove to be more of a challenge than any of the other recent victims, and her death would even provide a kind of vengeance for Ingram's death.

It had to be her. She was the perfect choice.

Paige found a number for the prison and called.

"Hi," she said, when she got through. "This is Paige King. I was there with Agent Marriott of the FBI to interrogate Lars Ingram."

"How can we help you, Agent King?" a man's voice on the other end of the line asked.

Paige didn't correct him on that, simply because there wasn't any time to waste. Besides, it might mean that he was more inclined to help.

"I believe that one of your guards may be in danger. I only have a first name: Nadia. She works on death row and was present at Lars Ingram's execution. I believe that the copycat killer we're hunting may be about to target her."

"That would be Nadia Stafford."

"I need contact information for her," Paige said. She hoped that she would be able to get in touch in time. "Urgently."

Her tone must have convinced the man on the end of the line of the seriousness of the situation, because it was only a moment or two before he came back with a number and an address.

"Thank you," Paige said, and hung up.

The first thing she did was to try to call Nadia to warn her, but that went straight through to voicemail.

"Nadia, this is Dr. Paige King, the consultant with the FBI who came to question Lars Ingram. I believe that you may be the next target of Ingram's copycat. Call me back as soon as you get this."

Paige's next call was to Christopher, but there was no answer. She guessed that he was still stuck in his interrogation of Cal Sanders, trying to get answers out of him.

"Christopher," Paige said as it went through to his voicemail. "Look, I know we didn't agree earlier, but please, just listen to me. I think I know where the killer is going to strike next. I'm on my way there now. The guard who took Ingram to his execution: Nadia Stafford. I'll text you her address."

Paige hung up and texted the address as she'd promised, then ran for her car. The sooner she got there, the better. It was getting dark outside as Paige sprinted from her apartment block, not wanting to waste a second if she could avoid it.

Should she call the D.C. police? Should she call the main FBI switchboard? Maybe if she called in her suspicions, a squad car would be able to get to Nadia Stafford's home quicker than she could. If they acted quickly, they could have a whole tactical team waiting when the killer showed up.

Paige didn't do that, though, because she wasn't sure right then if anyone would believe her. This was still just a hunch, so if she called it in and they asked for evidence, what would she be able to say? If she *did* get backup and then nothing happened, why would anyone ever trust her judgement again. No, this was something she had to do alone, at least until she knew more. If she *was* right, though, then she needed to get to Nadia Stafford's house as soon as possible.

*

The house was a tall, three-story building, run down and not in the best neighborhood of the city. Paige guessed that working as a prison guard wasn't the highest paid job out there.

For now, though, it was Nadia's safety that Paige was worried about, not where she lived. Parking as close as she could to the building, Paige ran up to the front door and held her finger down on the doorbell, hoping that she'd gotten there in time.

It was at least a minute before Paige got any kind of answer. Then, the voice of the guard came through an intercom.

"Yes, what is it?" She sounded annoyed at being disturbed.

"Nadia, this is Paige King, from the prison. I'm here because I believe that you might be in danger."

"Paige King?" There was a pause, presumably as Nadia remembered who she was. "What do you mean 'I might be in danger?'"

"Let me in and I'll explain," Maya said.

It was another moment or two before the guard opened the door. Now that she was at home, she was dressed in jeans, a light blue t-shirt and a plaid shirt. Her expression was obviously concerned.

"Ok, come in. You'd better tell me what's going on."

Nadia led the way through to a living room that looked as if it had been furnished out of an IKEA catalogue, with everything neat but slightly impersonal, as if she didn't spend enough time there to want to make it more her own. Or maybe she just didn't care about the look of the place so long as it was comfortable and worked well. She gestured for Paige to take a seat.

"All right," Nadia said. "What's all of this about? And why are you here alone? You were with that FBI agent before, Agent Marriott?"

Paige nodded. "I've tried to get through to him to let him know what's happening, but I didn't want to wait for him to get back to me before I came to warn you."

"Warn me about what?" Nadia asked. "You're acting like I'm in danger."

"I think you might be," Paige said. "I believe that the copycat killer might be about to target you."

Paige could see the shock on the other woman's face. "What? But that makes no sense."

Paige shook her head. "I think to him, it will make a lot of sense. I think that your job will technically fit into the victim profile that he uses, you're a woman of the right age, and he will want someone with a strong connection to Lars Ingram for his next victim, as a way of marking Ingram's death."

She knew how thin it all had to sound, but when dealing with a serial killer like this, that kind of reasoning would be more than enough for him to try to kill Nadia.

"That's..." Nadia looked around, her nerves obvious. "I kind of want to make sure that all the doors and windows are shut, now you've said that."

"That's probably a good idea," Paige said. "Have you seen any sign of anyone near here who shouldn't be here?"

"No," Nadia said. "But then, it's not like I've been looking for anything suspicious. Look, I'm going to check the back door. Are you *sure* about all this?"

That was the problem: Paige couldn't be truly certain about any of it. This was just her best guess, based on what she thought the killer wanted to achieve with this murder spree. It fit the pattern, but for all Paige knew, he could be somewhere else, trying to murder an ordinary overnight caretaker or au pair.

"I'm not certain," Paige said, "but I can't think of anyone else he would want to kill more right now."

She saw Nadia shudder at that. Nadia moved off towards what had to be a kitchen, presumably to go check the back door to the house. Paige went to go with her, not wanting her to be alone until they were sure the house was safe.

That was when Christopher called her. Paige answered immediately.

"Paige, where are you?" he asked.

"I'm at Nadia Stafford's house," she said.

"Because you think a killer is going there?"

"I know you think it's Cal Sanders, but I really think this is where the killer is going to strike next," Paige said.

"So you went there, alone?" She could hear the disapproval in his voice. "And is there any sign of anyone?"

"Not yet, but-"

Paige stopped, because that was the moment a terrified, pained scream came from the kitchen. It was Nadia's voice.

The killer was there.

CHAPTER TWENTY NINE

Paige ran into the kitchen, wishing in that moment that she'd graduated from the FBI academy, and that she was a fully armed FBI agent. As it was, she was unarmed when she burst in there only to find Nadia grappling with a black clad man, fighting for her life.

He was around six feet tall, broad shouldered, but not so massively built that he would stand out in a crowd. He had dark hair and was clean shaven. He was wearing black gloves that probably accounted for the lack of fingerprints at any of the crime scenes. His expression was one of pure, focused fury, while in his right hand Paige saw the steel flash of a knife.

The strangest thing was that Paige had a flash of recognition then. She'd seen him before, in the crowd at the execution. She'd assumed that he was a lawyer or a family member, but instead, the killer had been right there.

Nadia was trying to fight him off, but Paige could see blood on her arms where she'd been cut. If Paige didn't help, there was no way that she would last much longer.

In that moment, Paige's mind flashed back to the academy, to her training drills in unarmed combat. She thought of all the times she'd gotten it wrong against an instructor, all the times she'd been stabbed in practice. That had been a dummy knife, though. She'd been able to stop and start again, with no damage to anything but her pride. *This* knife looked wickedly sharp.

Even so, Paige threw herself into the fray, trying to help Nadia to get control of the attacker, trying to stop him from hurting either of them.

She grabbed for him, then had to dodge back as the knife came slashing for her. She managed to get a grip on the knife arm the second time it came for her, and again her mind flashed back to the training room.

"You have to be more aggressive, King. You have to take down the suspect, not wait for him to kill you."

Paige struck out with her knees and feet, trying to distract the killer from his grip on the knife long enough to wrench it from his grasp.

149

Nadia came in from his side, but he kicked her in the stomach hard enough that she doubled up with it, the air rushing out of her.

Even as she pushed her way back to her feet, the killer focused his attentions on Paige, hitting her hard with his free hand in the ribs, then shoving her away so that she went stumbling into a stack of dishes waiting to be washed up.

Paige spotted a cast iron skillet there among the plates and the cutlery. She grabbed for it, bringing it around just in time to block another strike by the knife. The killer spun towards Nadia again then, but Paige brought the skillet down hard on his arm, making him cry out in pain and drop it. The knife clattered as it hit the floor, spinning away from the three of them.

Nadia moved in, as if she might tackle the killer then, but he stepped back, blocking the rush. He hit her hard with his fist, then his elbow, and Paige saw Nadia go down, obviously stunned. The killer kicked her with a booted foot as she fell, and she slumped fully into unconsciousness.

Paige leapt at him, trying to use her improvised weapon to attack, but the killer was there, slamming into her and wrenching the skillet from Paige's hand with a savage strength she couldn't hope to match. She jabbed upwards at his jaw with her palm, then stomped down at his foot with her heel. The blows did *something,* but not nearly enough. He shoved her back, again with more strength than Paige could hope to match, and for a second or two they were apart from one another.

The knife was there on the floor, between them, gleaming with a deadly shine. Paige wasn't sure which of them would get there first if they both dove for it, but the killer had already shown just how dangerous he was when it came to a fight.

"I'm FBI," Paige said. "We know who you are. This is done."

"And yet you're here alone, Paige King," he replied, in a dangerous tone. He must have seen her look of surprise in that moment. "Oh, yes, I know who you are. I saw you on the news. You and that agent, running around, trying to catch up to me."

"And now we have," Paige said. "You must know that this is over. Even if you kill this woman, we know who you are now. You won't get away."

"And yet you haven't used my name," the killer said. "Which makes me think that you don't know as much as you're pretending."

Paige knew in that moment that she had to keep him talking, had to try to delay, to string this out. If she could get him to keep talking long enough, then she might be able to think of a way out of this situation, or help might arrive. If she couldn't…

She glanced down at the knife. If she couldn't keep him talking, then it was going to be a race to see who got to it first.

"What *is* your name?" Paige asked.

He didn't answer at first, but then shrugged.

"Carmichael," he said. "Sebastian Carmichael."

The fact that he was willing to tell Paige that said to her exactly how he thought that this was going to end. He thought that he was going to kill her, and Paige couldn't help feeling a deep rush of terror at the thought that he might be right. She'd tried fighting him, and it was obvious that he was stronger.

She needed to find a way to catch him off guard if she was going to have a chance, and she needed to find another weapon.

"Maybe you're right," Paige said. "Maybe I don't know as much about you as I should. But then, you're just a copycat killer, aren't you?"

This was a very dangerous tactic, one deliberately calculated to anger an already dangerous man. The fact was that if he stayed cold and calculating, Sebastian Carmichael was going to be able to kill Paige easily. Paige had felt how much stronger than her he was. She needed him not to focus.

"If you think I'm just a copycat, then you really haven't been paying attention," Sebastian said.

"Oh, we know a lot," Paige said. "We know about Nikki Ashenko, for example. That was kind of a mess, wasn't it, Sebastian? But then, it was your first kill, wasn't it?"

He looked slightly surprised that she'd figured that part out. Paige's eyes were less on him, and more on the rest of the kitchen. There was a rack of knives on a countertop to her right. They seemed like a much better option than the one on the floor.

"And then you went on, copying Lars Ingram every time he killed, his shadow, his echo."

"That wasn't how it was," Sebastian said. No, Paige knew that it wasn't, but every extra second she bought, every fraction that she broke his concentration, was to her advantage. "I was his equal, his competitor."

"And yet you never did anything greater than he did," Paige said. "You only ever copied. You never did anything original."

151

"I've killed as many as he did. When I kill the pair of you, I'll have won."

Paige forced herself to smile in spite of the fear that she felt in that moment.

"You haven't won anything, Sebastian. If you're remembered at all, it will be as a footnote to Lars Ingram's crimes. Kill as many people as you want, but you'll still just be a bad copy."

"You bitch!" he snarled, his composure cracking.

Paige saw her opportunity. She lunged towards the knife on the floor, but it was a feint. She kicked it away even as Sebastian grabbed for it, and then made a second lunge, towards the knife rack on the side. She grabbed a kitchen knife, close to six inches long and obviously just as sharp as the one the killer had brought. She spun towards Carmichael, and now he had the blade in his hands, squaring off against Paige.

There was no room to circle and dodge in the kitchen, no room for cleverness or trickery. Paige had seen in the training room what fights involving knives could be like.

She just had to hope that she was up to this one.

She slashed at Carmichael as he got too close, making him jump back. She feinted another slash, then pulled back as Carmichael struck out at her arm, missing her by inches.

"It's a standoff, Sebastian," she said. "You can't get close without me stabbing you, and you don't dare turn your back to run. So we just wait now, for help to arrive."

He snarled then and lunged forward in spite of Paige's warning. She got a clean cut in on his chest, but then he was in close trying to stab at her in return. Paige managed to get a hand on his knife arm, but his own meaty hand closed over the wrist of the hand with which she held the knife.

They were pressed in close together then, close enough that Paige could smell the fresh blood on him and the scent of sweat. Close enough that they could both strike at each other with head and knee and shoulder. The blows were battering, bruising, but Paige clung onto Carmichael for her life, knowing that if she lost her grip on the knife arm even for a moment, she was going to die.

The only problem was the killer's sheer strength. His grip felt as if it were grinding the bones of her wrist together, twisting with an awful power that meant that Paige simply couldn't keep her grip on the knife she held. She heard the rattle of the metal as it tumbled to the kitchen floor, and now it was just her fighting for her life against a knife again.

Desperation gave her strength. Paige threw a headbutt that cracked into Carmichael's nose. That let her wrench free of the grip on her now free arm, so that she could lock onto the knife arm with everything she had, keeping the knife trapped, making it impossible for Carmichael to get a real thrust in.

"You might as well give up," he said. "You can't hang on forever, and then..."

Even as he said it, Paige saw Nadia rise up unsteadily from the floor, obviously starting to recover her wits after being knocked out. She grabbed the knife that was down there, and stabbed with it, driving it deep into the shoulder of Carmichael's knife arm before collapsing back to her knees as if that had taken all of her strength.

Carmichael screamed in a mixture of rage and pain, wrenching back from Paige even as he dropped the knife in his agony.

Don't stop. Keep fighting.

Her instructor's words echoed in Paige's memory as she charged forward, hitting out at Carmichael with everything she had. She kicked him in the knee, hard, then brought her elbow up sharply into his jaw. As he rocked back, she tripped him, sending him tumbling to the floor.

She and Nadia both grabbed for him then, and now that it was two against one again with no weapon, they had the advantage. Carmichael was still strong, still bucking with all the violence he had, but he was also crying out in agony as he did it, the blade embedded in his shoulder taking much of the fight out of him.

Paige wrenched him over onto his stomach. She didn't have any handcuffs, but at least she could hold him there where he couldn't do any more harm to her or Nadia.

Almost distantly, she heard the crack of a door breaking, followed by the sound of feet running towards her. Christopher burst into the kitchen then, gun already out in his hand, face ashen with worry.

"I heard the scream and I thought... Are you all right, Paige?"

"I'm fine," Paige said, although in truth, she wasn't sure how badly she was hurt. She was pretty sure that Carmichael must have cut her at some point in the fight, but pure adrenaline stopped her from feeling it.

She nodded down at Carmichael.

"This is Sebastian Carmichael, the copycat killer. We've done it, Christopher. We've caught him."

CHAPTER THIRTY

Paige could see the surprise on Christopher's face as he stood there, watching her and Nadia hold down Sebastian Carmichael. Then he rushed forward, taking out handcuffs to secure him.

"This is the killer," Paige said. "Not Cal Sanders."

"And while I was stuck in an interrogation trying to get a confession out of the wrong man, you were here taking on the real killer alone," Christopher said. He sounded slightly guilty about that. "You shouldn't have had to do that."

"I had help," Paige said, with a nod across to Nadia. She was convinced that the prison guard's toughness was one of the main things that had made this turn out better than all the other times Carmichael had attacked women. It was what had allowed her to survive those seconds that it took for Paige to get there.

"I should still have been here," Christopher said. He took out his phone, making a call. "This is Agent Marriott. I'm going to need an ambulance on site at my location. I have a prisoner with a knife wound, and a civilian who looks as though she has suffered cuts to her arms." He looked over to Paige. "Paige, are you injured?"

Paige could hear the concern there, and she realized that she didn't know. She started to look over her arms and her stomach, knowing from her training that it was far too easy for someone to get stabbed in a fight without realizing it, the adrenaline of the fight covering the pain of it.

"Here, let me," Christopher said, moving around Paige to check her for injuries. It felt strange having him so close, checking over her body like that. It was hard to keep from reacting to that closeness, especially when he was in front of her, looking into her eyes, just inches away.

Paige had to remind herself that there wasn't anything between them, that there couldn't be. That this was just him checking to see if she was all right and nothing more, and that anything she felt right then was probably just the emotional aftereffect of being in such a dangerous situation and surviving. Even so, she wanted nothing more in that moment than to close the distance between them, to throw her arms around him at least. It took everything Paige had not to do it.

"I think you've suffered some minor cuts," he said, "but nothing serious. I still want you to get checked over at the hospital, though."

"What about me?" Sebastian Carmichael demanded, in an agonized voice. "I have a *knife* in my *shoulder*."

"That will have to stay in until it can be removed professionally," Christopher said. "We wouldn't want to kill you accidentally. Not before your trial and conviction for four murders."

"More than that," Paige said.

Christopher looked over at her sharply. "More?"

"By my count, almost half of the murders attributed to Lars Ingram were actually down to Sebastian here. By today, they had as many kills as each other." After all he'd done, Paige couldn't stop herself from kneeling down in front of Carmichael, exacting the one piece of revenge that she knew would hurt the most.

"You almost won, Sebastian, but you failed."

He'd failed, and with any luck, he would go down in history as nothing more than a copycat. He wouldn't get the recognition for his crimes that he so obviously craved. There would be attention for a little while, of course, but after that, Paige hoped that he wouldn't be remembered as anything other than someone trying to copy Lars Ingram, if he was remembered at all.

"Paige, can I talk to you for a moment?" Christopher asked.

Paige nodded, and he led the way out of the kitchen. Paige had no worries about Carmichael trying to escape. If anyone could restrain a handcuffed prisoner, it was a trained prison guard.

"What is it?" Paige asked. In spite of herself, a part of her still hoped that he would say how worried he'd been about her, or that the danger of all of this had made him realize that he had feelings for her.

"I wanted to apologize," he said. "I shouldn't have spoken to you the way I did outside the interrogation room. I should have listened to you. My instincts had me in there with a man determined not to say anything. Yours caught a killer."

"*We* caught a killer," Paige said. "I wouldn't even be on this case if you hadn't believed in me."

"Well, I'm glad that I did, or we might have had another death on our hands," Christopher said. "You'll make an amazing agent, Paige."

Paige hoped so, she really did.

*

Graduating from the FBI academy was a big deal, and not just because of the effort it represented in getting to this point. The whole class was there, out in front of the main administrative building of the compound, but so were plenty of other people. It seemed that everyone had friends or family who wanted to see them in this moment, so that the space in front of the low stage that had been set up was thronged with people.

Almost astonishingly, Paige actually had someone there for her. Her mother had come, sitting a couple of rows back from the front, looking incredibly proud even if Paige suspected that she still didn't quite understand Paige's decision to work with the FBI like this.

Christopher was there too, looking almost as proud as Paige's mother did. Maybe he would have come anyway, but Paige wanted to believe that he was there for her.

The ceremony began, with Agent Podovski moving out to the front of the stage to speak.

"I still remember when I first became an FBI agent," he said. "I thought that it would be like something from TV, all running around, chases and shooting suspects. Solving crimes with brilliant deduction, sweating suspects until they finally cracked. When I came through the academy and joined the bureau, I discovered that... well, yes, all of those things could and did happen. But they weren't the most important part of what we did to catch criminals and protect the US from domestic threats."

He gestured to where Paige and the others waited by the side of the stage, ready to walk up and collect the diplomas that would formally mark their completion of the course.

"The part that mattered was the teamwork," Agent Podovski said. "You will be working with people in potentially dangerous situations, to catch very dangerous people. You will have to rely on them not just to play their part in every case, but to have your back when you need it. That is the reason why we hold you all to high standards here at the academy: not because we want people who will make superb agents, but because we want people out in the field we would trust to have our backs. All of you here today have met that standard. You should be proud, both of yourselves and of each other."

He started to call out the names of the students, and one by one they walked up to receive their diplomas. Paige found herself waiting, applauding each of the students in turn as they made their transition from trainees to qualified agents. She'd attended graduations for high school, for her degree, for her MA, and for her PhD, yet somehow, this one felt more meaningful than all the rest of them.

"Paige King!"

Paige marched up onto the stage after the others, taking her diploma, receiving the briefest of handshakes, and taking the time to look across to where her mother was beaming with pride. Christopher was on his feet, applauding. Paige felt almost as grateful for that as for her mother's presence.

She marched down off the far side of the stage and waited for the rest to finish collecting their diplomas. Agent Podovski stepped forward again.

"Thank you to everyone here. I hope that you will all help to make this country a safer place and make the FBI proud."

Paige was able to head out into the crowd now, seeking out her mother and hugging her tightly. She looked around, and Christopher was there, holding out a hand for her to shake. Paige wanted so much more than that. She wanted to hug him tightly, at the very least.

Then she saw the woman standing by his side, lovely and dark haired, with a gentle smile and deep brown eyes.

"You must be Paige," she said. "Christopher has told me so much about you. I'm so glad that I get to finally meet you."

Paige realized who this had to be.

"Justine?"

"Ah, so Christopher *has* mentioned me."

"It's good to meet you," Paige said, although she wasn't sure if it was true. The problem was simple: this woman seemed *nice*, and Paige didn't want Christopher's wife to be nice. That just made her feel guilty for every feeling that she had.

Justine hugged her where her husband couldn't. "Congratulations. I don't know exactly what it means to be an agent, but I know how much it means to Christopher. I hope you get to do everything you want to in the FBI."

"Actually, that reminds me," Christopher said. "My boss is here somewhere. Agent Sauer wants to talk to you."

That caught Paige a little by surprise. Why would Christopher's boss want to talk to her? She looked around until she spotted him a little way off in the crowd and went over to him.

"Agent Sauer?" she said. "You wanted to talk to me?"

He looked around at her, and to Paige's surprise, he smiled.

157

"Ah, there you are. I want to start by apologizing for the way I was when I first met you. I hope you understand that I just wanted to make sure that the best people possible were on the copycat case."

"I understand," Paige said.

"But it turns out that you *were* the best person for the job," Agent Sauer said. "And this is the second serial killer you've helped to bring to justice. That's why I want to offer you a job."

"A job?" Paige said. She hadn't expected it to be that easy.

"I think you would fit in well in the Behavioral Analysis Unit. Specifically, I believe that Agent Marriott needs a partner, and that you would fit that role very well."

Paige was stunned by the offer. It was the kind of thing that she knew she should have jumped at, excitement overwhelming her. She should have accepted instantly, but the truth was that it wasn't that simple. Given her feelings towards Christopher, was it really safe to accept a job working so closely with him?

"I... I need to think about it," she said. "It's all pretty overwhelming."

"Of course," Agent Sauer said. He pressed a card into her hand. "Let me know any time in the next couple of days."

"I will, sir," Paige promised, although she didn't know right then exactly what she was going to say to him.

*

Paige sat in her apartment, truly home again for the first time in a long time. She was eating pizza and drinking beer, trying to make up her mind what she was going to say to Agent Sauer. She *wanted* the job, but could she really risk taking it?

Paige was still trying to make up her mind when the news came on her TV. Paige wasn't watching it closely, but the moment a headline came up on the screen, Paige couldn't look away.

Exsanguination Killer Claims Another Victim.

"A body was found today in Virginia, killed in a manner that the local police are saying is consistent with notorious serial killer the Exsanguination Killer. The police aren't releasing details at this time but say that inquiries are continuing."

Paige wanted to know *what* inquiries, and even as she thought it, she knew that she had a way to find out. As an FBI agent, she could find out more. She might finally be in a position to actually learn what had happened to her father. And the *best* way to do that was probably from inside the BAU.

She might become an agent somewhere else, but if she was sent to a field office in another city, she wouldn't have a chance to look into this. She had to be here, in D.C., in the BAU.

Picking up her phone, she called Agent Sauer.

"Agent Sauer? This is Paige King. I'm just calling to say... I accept."

Whatever it took, she would find answers when it came to her father's death.

NOW AVAILABLE!

THE GIRL HE TOOK
(A Paige King FBI Suspense Thriller—Book 3)

Paige King, a Ph.D. in forensic psychology and a new arrival at the FBI's elite BAU unit, has an uncanny ability to enter serial killers' minds. She has seen the worst of the worst—but when a new serial killer strikes, victims turning up dead with magic tricks left at the scenes, Paige is baffled. What could the meaning be behind these macabre hints?

"A masterpiece of thriller and mystery."
—Books and Movie Reviews, Roberto Mattos (re *Once Gone*)

THE GIRL HE TOOK is book #3 in a new series by #1 bestselling and critically acclaimed mystery and suspense author Blake Pierce.

Up against her most challenging case yet, Paige must use her encyclopedic knowledge to decode the meaning of the strange magic clues. Can she discover what the killer wants, and why?

Or by the time she figures it out, will it be too late?

A complex psychological crime thriller full of twists and turns and packed with heart-pounding suspense, the PAIGE KING mystery series will make you fall in love with a brilliant new female protagonist and keep you turning pages late into the night.

Books #4-#6 are also available!

"An edge of your seat thriller in a new series that keeps you turning pages! ...So many twists, turns and red herrings... I can't wait to see what happens next."
—Reader review (*Her Last Wish*)

"A strong, complex story about two FBI agents trying to stop a serial killer. If you want an author to capture your attention and have you guessing, yet trying to put the pieces together, Pierce is your author!"
—Reader review (*Her Last Wish*)

"A typical Blake Pierce twisting, turning, roller coaster ride suspense thriller. Will have you turning the pages to the last sentence of the last chapter!!!"
—Reader review (*City of Prey*)

"Right from the start we have an unusual protagonist that I haven't seen done in this genre before. The action is nonstop... A very atmospheric novel that will keep you turning pages well into the wee hours."
—Reader review (*City of Prey*)

"Everything that I look for in a book... a great plot, interesting characters, and grabs your interest right away. The book moves along at a breakneck pace and stays that way until the end. Now on go I to book two!"
—Reader review (*Girl, Alone*)

"Exciting, heart pounding, edge of your seat book... a must read for mystery and suspense readers!"
—Reader review (*Girl, Alone*)

Blake Pierce

Blake Pierce is the USA Today bestselling author of the RILEY PAGE mystery series, which includes seventeen books. Blake Pierce is also the author of the MACKENZIE WHITE mystery series, comprising fourteen books; of the AVERY BLACK mystery series, comprising six books; of the KERI LOCKE mystery series, comprising five books; of the MAKING OF RILEY PAIGE mystery series, comprising six books; of the KATE WISE mystery series, comprising seven books; of the CHLOE FINE psychological suspense mystery, comprising six books; of the JESSE HUNT psychological suspense thriller series, comprising twenty four books; of the AU PAIR psychological suspense thriller series, comprising three books; of the ZOE PRIME mystery series, comprising six books; of the ADELE SHARP mystery series, comprising fifteen books, of the EUROPEAN VOYAGE cozy mystery series, comprising four books; of the new LAURA FROST FBI suspense thriller, comprising nine books (and counting); of the new ELLA DARK FBI suspense thriller, comprising eleven books (and counting); of the A YEAR IN EUROPE cozy mystery series, comprising nine books, of the AVA GOLD mystery series, comprising six books (and counting); of the RACHEL GIFT mystery series, comprising six books (and counting); of the VALERIE LAW mystery series, comprising three books (and counting); of the PAIGE KING mystery series, comprising six books (and counting); and of the MAY MOORE suspense thriller series, comprising three books (and counting).

An avid reader and lifelong fan of the mystery and thriller genres, Blake loves to hear from you, so please feel free to visit www.blakepierceauthor.com to learn more and stay in touch.

BOOKS BY BLAKE PIERCE

PAIGE KING MYSTERY SERIES
THE GIRL HE PINED (Book #1)
THE GIRL HE CHOSE (Book #2)
THE GIRL HE TOOK (Book #3)

VALERIE LAW MYSTERY SERIES
NO MERCY (Book #1)
NO PITY (Book #2)
NO FEAR (Book #3

RACHEL GIFT MYSTERY SERIES
HER LAST WISH (Book #1)
HER LAST CHANCE (Book #2)
HER LAST HOPE (Book #3)
HER LAST FEAR (Book #4)
HER LAST CHOICE (Book #5)
HER LAST BREATH (Book #6)

AVA GOLD MYSTERY SERIES
CITY OF PREY (Book #1)
CITY OF FEAR (Book #2)
CITY OF BONES (Book #3)
CITY OF GHOSTS (Book #4)
CITY OF DEATH (Book #5)
CITY OF VICE (Book #6)

A YEAR IN EUROPE
A MURDER IN PARIS (Book #1)
DEATH IN FLORENCE (Book #2)
VENGEANCE IN VIENNA (Book #3)
A FATALITY IN SPAIN (Book #4)

ELLA DARK FBI SUSPENSE THRILLER
GIRL, ALONE (Book #1)

GIRL, TAKEN (Book #2)
GIRL, HUNTED (Book #3)
GIRL, SILENCED (Book #4)
GIRL, VANISHED (Book 5)
GIRL ERASED (Book #6)
GIRL, FORSAKEN (Book #7)
GIRL, TRAPPED (Book #8)
GIRL, EXPENDABLE (Book #9)
GIRL, ESCAPED (Book #10)
GIRL, HIS (Book #11)

LAURA FROST FBI SUSPENSE THRILLER
ALREADY GONE (Book #1)
ALREADY SEEN (Book #2)
ALREADY TRAPPED (Book #3)
ALREADY MISSING (Book #4)
ALREADY DEAD (Book #5)
ALREADY TAKEN (Book #6)
ALREADY CHOSEN (Book #7)
ALREADY LOST (Book #8)
ALREADY HIS (Book #9)

EUROPEAN VOYAGE COZY MYSTERY SERIES
MURDER (AND BAKLAVA) (Book #1)
DEATH (AND APPLE STRUDEL) (Book #2)
CRIME (AND LAGER) (Book #3)
MISFORTUNE (AND GOUDA) (Book #4)
CALAMITY (AND A DANISH) (Book #5)
MAYHEM (AND HERRING) (Book #6)

ADELE SHARP MYSTERY SERIES
LEFT TO DIE (Book #1)
LEFT TO RUN (Book #2)
LEFT TO HIDE (Book #3)
LEFT TO KILL (Book #4)
LEFT TO MURDER (Book #5)
LEFT TO ENVY (Book #6)
LEFT TO LAPSE (Book #7)
LEFT TO VANISH (Book #8)

LEFT TO HUNT (Book #9)
LEFT TO FEAR (Book #10)
LEFT TO PREY (Book #11)
LEFT TO LURE (Book #12)
LEFT TO CRAVE (Book #13)
LEFT TO LOATHE (Book #14)
LEFT TO HARM (Book #15)

THE AU PAIR SERIES
ALMOST GONE (Book#1)
ALMOST LOST (Book #2)
ALMOST DEAD (Book #3)

ZOE PRIME MYSTERY SERIES
FACE OF DEATH (Book#1)
FACE OF MURDER (Book #2)
FACE OF FEAR (Book #3)
FACE OF MADNESS (Book #4)
FACE OF FURY (Book #5)
FACE OF DARKNESS (Book #6)

A JESSIE HUNT PSYCHOLOGICAL SUSPENSE SERIES
THE PERFECT WIFE (Book #1)
THE PERFECT BLOCK (Book #2)
THE PERFECT HOUSE (Book #3)
THE PERFECT SMILE (Book #4)
THE PERFECT LIE (Book #5)
THE PERFECT LOOK (Book #6)
THE PERFECT AFFAIR (Book #7)
THE PERFECT ALIBI (Book #8)
THE PERFECT NEIGHBOR (Book #9)
THE PERFECT DISGUISE (Book #10)
THE PERFECT SECRET (Book #11)
THE PERFECT FAÇADE (Book #12)
THE PERFECT IMPRESSION (Book #13)
THE PERFECT DECEIT (Book #14)
THE PERFECT MISTRESS (Book #15)
THE PERFECT IMAGE (Book #16)
THE PERFECT VEIL (Book #17)

THE PERFECT INDISCRETION (Book #18)
THE PERFECT RUMOR (Book #19)
THE PERFECT COUPLE (Book #20)
THE PERFECT MURDER (Book #21)
THE PERFECT HUSBAND (Book #22)
THE PERFECT SCANDAL (Book #23)
THE PERFECT MASK (Book #24)

CHLOE FINE PSYCHOLOGICAL SUSPENSE SERIES
NEXT DOOR (Book #1)
A NEIGHBOR'S LIE (Book #2)
CUL DE SAC (Book #3)
SILENT NEIGHBOR (Book #4)
HOMECOMING (Book #5)
TINTED WINDOWS (Book #6)

KATE WISE MYSTERY SERIES
IF SHE KNEW (Book #1)
IF SHE SAW (Book #2)
IF SHE RAN (Book #3)
IF SHE HID (Book #4)
IF SHE FLED (Book #5)
IF SHE FEARED (Book #6)
IF SHE HEARD (Book #7)

THE MAKING OF RILEY PAIGE SERIES
WATCHING (Book #1)
WAITING (Book #2)
LURING (Book #3)
TAKING (Book #4)
STALKING (Book #5)
KILLING (Book #6)

RILEY PAIGE MYSTERY SERIES
ONCE GONE (Book #1)
ONCE TAKEN (Book #2)
ONCE CRAVED (Book #3)
ONCE LURED (Book #4)

ONCE HUNTED (Book #5)
ONCE PINED (Book #6)
ONCE FORSAKEN (Book #7)
ONCE COLD (Book #8)
ONCE STALKED (Book #9)
ONCE LOST (Book #10)
ONCE BURIED (Book #11)
ONCE BOUND (Book #12)
ONCE TRAPPED (Book #13)
ONCE DORMANT (Book #14)
ONCE SHUNNED (Book #15)
ONCE MISSED (Book #16)
ONCE CHOSEN (Book #17)

MACKENZIE WHITE MYSTERY SERIES
BEFORE HE KILLS (Book #1)
BEFORE HE SEES (Book #2)
BEFORE HE COVETS (Book #3)
BEFORE HE TAKES (Book #4)
BEFORE HE NEEDS (Book #5)
BEFORE HE FEELS (Book #6)
BEFORE HE SINS (Book #7)
BEFORE HE HUNTS (Book #8)
BEFORE HE PREYS (Book #9)
BEFORE HE LONGS (Book #10)
BEFORE HE LAPSES (Book #11)
BEFORE HE ENVIES (Book #12)
BEFORE HE STALKS (Book #13)
BEFORE HE HARMS (Book #14)

AVERY BLACK MYSTERY SERIES
CAUSE TO KILL (Book #1)
CAUSE TO RUN (Book #2)
CAUSE TO HIDE (Book #3)
CAUSE TO FEAR (Book #4)
CAUSE TO SAVE (Book #5)
CAUSE TO DREAD (Book #6)

KERI LOCKE MYSTERY SERIES

Made in the USA
Las Vegas, NV
13 May 2024

89884442R00098